The Essence
of
Numerology

Other books by the author

The Tarot Power
The Power of Planets
The Essence of Astrology
Numerology & Sun Signs
Sun Signs
Power of Mantra and Yantra
Love Signs
Horoscope 2008 (also in Hindi)
Interpretation of Dreams

The Essence
of
Numerology

P. KHURRANA

Rupa & Co

Typeset in Goudy Old Style by
Mindways Design
1410 Chiranjiv Tower
43 Nehru Place
New Delhi 110 019

Printed in India by
Anubha Printers
B-48, Sector-7
Noida 201 301

*Those who know Astrology only indicate
in a way what will take place in future.
Who else, except the Creator Brahma,
can say with certainty what will definitely happen?*

To the memory of my
mother

Contents

Contents

Preface

The science of numbers or numerology is a fascinating and intriguing study. It predicts the future and one's personality using the foundation of numbers. As per the beliefs of many numerologists, the study of numbers has its philosophy, its alphabets, its language and all its terminology founded on the birth date and name of the individual.

Numerology is a heavenly subject; a universal law consists of nine numbers ie, 1 to 9 which affect one and shape one's future. It stands majestically on its own principles, whether one calls it fiction or mystic theory.

Numerology has been rationally used to determine one's nature and the direction of one's life. Each number represents a different character—the capacity for love, intelligence, work emotions and expressions.

One's birth number represents the complete character of a person. For example, a person born on 1, 10, 19 or 28 of any month shows originality, energy, enthusiasm, brilliance and intellectual characteristics. Number 1 symbolises the Sun which rules will power and ego. It is the core of one's potential and uniqueness as an individual.

One's birth number represents the main direction and focus one wants one's life to take and one's determination to accomplish what one sets out to do. It represents one's personal honesty and integrity, one's ability to command respect and authority, and one's capacity to impress and influence others.

In astrology, in order to gain a detailed insight into one's personality, a 'natal' horoscope or birth chart, is necessary. So a professional astrologer takes into account the position of all these 'planets' in the birth chart in a personal consultation, using only the time, date and place of birth. Similarly, numerology has greater accuracy which focuses on one's character, problems, and forecasts one's future choices and best and timely solutions to problems. It has many things to reveal about one's personality.

Most readers are wary of number 8 ie, Saturn. It is believed to be the number of death and destruction. But I take the opportunity to disagree with others numerologists. My research reveals that 8 is a number of truth and sacrifice and this was given to Lord Jesus Christ in His role as the redeemer of the world. This number reflects a deep and intense nature. It includes great strength and individuality, but is normally misunderstood. However, every number has its vices and virtues, but they vary from individual to individual. For example, number 2 is lucky for me, but is not necessary lucky for other individuals. This has been the case for every number, which has different mystic relations with every individual.

Numbers can affect the way one thinks and behaves when one associaties with another person. It can also provide one with fascinating information about complete characteristics of others. When one meets someone to whom one is attracted, numerology can provide one with a valuable insight into his or her personality. It may even reveal unattractive characteristics that one's prospective partner is trying to conceal.

Though the book is not a complete manual on numerology, it is my sincere attempt to give lay readers a chance to understand the role of their date of birth in the lives. The book contains all the necessary information pertaining to career, health, foreign travel; love and relationships, respective mantras, gems, lucky days, and colours. The book is a boon to people keen on getting acquainted with Numerology. They need not depend on any hearsay rules or come to wrong conclusions. The practitioner or the amateur can both profit from reading the book and will get many conceptions of the subject cleared. Every person is influenced by his 'destiny number', which tends to be a path to one's inner self. Let the 'destiny number' be one's guiding force and I am certain that one will become focused and strong, and this would lead to a complete change for the better as far as one's personality is concerned.

P. KHURRANA
Astrologer

OFFICE
Hotel Shivalikview,
Sector 17,
Chandigarh (India)
Ph: 2703018, 4644018
Website: www.astroindia.com
E-mail: pkhurrana@astroindia.com

Foreword

Ever since man stepped out of the cave, he has had a natural instinct to wonder about what is going to happen to him in the future. Throughout history, there has been no dearth of people; some gifted with special talents, other mere shysters who have been willing to cater to this natural fascination. And one of the many methods has been divination. And one of the many methods of divination used, has been numerology.

Lets get it straight; astrology is one thing and witchcraft is another. Similarly palmistry, phrenology, tasseography and spiritualism are totally separate. Of course, it is possible to study, combine and apply any or all of these occult subjects. Indeed, there are many forthright and talented fortune tellers, but the science of numbers is profound enough to demand serious attention.

Though numerology does not 'tell fortunes' in the popular sense, if is properly used, it offers us a chance to understand our own motivations better and can indicate certain cyclical trends which might affect us in the future.

Numerology is one of the oldest disciplines, and men of wisdom, intelligence and distinction have long confounded skeptics by attesting their high regard for its principles. May I leave it, then, to a few of these to tempt you further.

Ralph Waldo Emerson: *Astrology is astronomy brought to earth and applied to the affairs of men.*

Sir Francis Bacon: *The natures and dispositions of men are, not without truth, distinguished from the predominance of the planets & numbers.*

John Ruskin: *The greatness or smallness of man is, in the most conclusive sense, determined for him at his birth.*

Today, there are equally distinguished scientists as well as leading doctors, psychologists and academics who accept the value of numerology.

Numerology is a difficult, but a very interesting science, which requires devoted study in order to make use of it in the service of mankind.

One should not deny numerology because of one numerologist's wrong predictions, any more than one denies medicine because one doctor makes a mistake in a diagnosis.

Both are empirical sciences which should only be practised by competent people.

The incompetence in the first case merely makes one smile, in the latter, it may lead to a fatal mistake.

I am not the first, and I shall certainly not be the last, to make this exciting journey. Some of my discoveries one will find in this book, and if they tempt one to venture further than to treat the basic sun sign characteristics as fodder for parlour games, if they help one understand how the lessons of astrology may be turned to one's advantage, then perhaps, I will have succeeded in passing on a fascination for this most ancient science.

Five of our greatest scientists and astronomers, each hailed as a genius, Johannes Kepler, Sir Isaac Newton, Tycho Brahe, Nicolaus Copernicus and Galileo Galilei were also astrologers.

Today there are equally distinguished scientists as well as leading doctors, psychologists and academics who accept the value of astrology. The list of important contemporary figures is endless, but special mention must be made of Sigmund Freud and Carl Jung. Dr Jung not only believed that astrology has repeatedly led us back to the knowledge that character and destiny are dependent upon certain moments in time, but declared that it represented the summation of all psychological knowledge of antiquity.

Characteristics of Numbers
1–9

Number 1

Persons born on

1, 10, 19 or 28

1

Representing the chief planet among the nine planets, the Sun symbolises Number 1. This is a planet which is waterless, temperate and optimistic. Its colour is orange and domicile is in Leo, exile in Virgo, fall in Libra and exaltation at 19 degrees of Aries. Its elements are partly air and partly fire. The planet symbolises the leader, the husband, the father, and the political ruler. While the planet is slightly unproductive, it does have its angle of benefit as far as business ventures and matters of finance are concerned. This planet helps the native acquire the assistance and collaboration of powerful people. When the cards are read, it symbolises the Day since it gives radiation, prosperity and permanence.

It governs the metal gold and the day Sunday.

The planet plays a significant role on the heart and should be deemed as the Lord of Life (Hyleg) in the horoscope of the individual. The only exception being that the influence is very weak. The influence of the planet should be examined very closely with reference to health. The position of the planet in the horoscope is again of immense value, both from the perspective of its place in the house and that of the sign it occupies, since it corresponds to the ruler of the nativity.

The life of the natives would be a pivotal point for all those who come in contact with them. They will more often be the leader than the led. Power, authority, influence and control characterise them. Since they will hold positions of significance, there is a high possibility of them making many adversaries without even realising it.

Love Life

Creative and expressive, they wish to put their love into words and hence, will write letters, messages and even poetry dedicated to their beloved. The flip side is that they want the same amount of devotion and dedication from their lovers. It would be a good idea not to be too rigid in this expectation, since there is a very strong chance that their partners may not be endowed with the same expressiveness and creativity.

Their sense of creativity extends to wanting to fashion an aura of romance. Drama and the allure associated with it is what they want to generate in their relationship. The idea being that everyone should be able to see their relationship in all its grandeur and elegance. Everything that is associated with the emotion of love is appreciated by them. Small gestures, thoughtful gifts and warmth is what they crave for. If their partners are even slightly aloof, they become moody and depressed. However, when things return to normal, they bounce back to their normal sunny selves. This will however, not happen if they ever get the feeling that they are being taken for granted since their self-esteem is extremely high and they want their partners to value them equally.

They are persistent and determined when they fall in love. Also, they have the tendency to be possessive yet loyal and passionate. It is important for them to have absolute faith in their partners' loyalty and may even go to the extent of wanting to see it proven. This could mean that they want their partners to demonstrate fidelity and devotion time and again. Although they may seem tough and unbreakable, they are quite tender inside and also insecure to an extent. They could easily chew their nails about love and its implications without letting others even get a hint of their worries.

It is important that they do not become too possessive and demanding. People easily get tired of this and hence, they could face more failures in love than normal. They should also ensure that they do not hog all the attention they get. They should develop the habit of sharing and then will find that being a couple becomes much easier. The true meaning of togetherness is being able to give and let go. Taking all the attention is an indication of self-centeredness and it would only result in negativity and hurt.

Finance and Profession

They have the full potential and the capability of making money. They may have to meet with hardship and difficulties in early years, but have every prospect of becoming well off and being able to gain power and position in any community.

Their career will be divided as it were into zones; upto about thirty-seven years, plenty of hard work will be required in overcoming difficulties; from thirty-seven onwards, they are likely to become, more or less prosperous and successful. Number 1 is the number of a successful taxing profession. We also find painters, jewellers, astrologers, sportsmen and generally people connected with high quality work. They are enthusiastic and careful about money.

Persons born on 1, 10, 19, or 28 will good **educators,** politicians, occupy high positions in the government; they possess excellent executive ability, and will be good managers of big concerns or corporation, directors, captains, sales managers etc.

Health and Food

In their childhood and early years, they will be liable to have many minor illnesses, especially fevers, rheumatism, inflammation of the blood veins, carbuncles and boils. But as they become older, that they will grow out of such problems, and become healthy and vigorous.

The spirit, the heart, and many a times the eyes, are weak health areas. They should not tax their nerves and energy reserves. Sometimes the solar-plexus can malfunction.

FAVOURABLE FOODS:
- Lemons
- Coconut
- Lichi
- Honey
- Green vegetables

UNFAVOURABLE FOODS:
- Red meat

• Lucky Numbers • Days • Alphabets • Colours

LUCKY NUMBERS AND DATES	All series of 1 and 4 10, 19, 28, 37, 46, 55, 4, 13, 22, 31, 40, 49
LUCKY DAY	Sunday
LUCKY ALPHABETS	M, T
LUCKY COLOURS	Red, orange and white
LUCKY GEMS	Ruby or amber
LUCKY TALISMAN	Sun in gold to be worn next to skin
LUCKY FLOWER	Red rose, sunflower, rosemary

MANTRA

Aum hran hrin hron sei: suryaye nameh

Number 2

Persons born on
2, 11, 20 or 29

2

The planet Moon represents number 2. This planet symbolises all material things. Its domicile is in Cancer; its exaltation at the degree of Taurus and its fall is in Scorpio. It is frosty, damp, variable, nocturnal and womanly.

When we begin to understand and analyse it, the planet is perceived as the mother. It is also a symbol of fortune, the unknown, travel, heritage, and transformation from a spiritual point of view.

This planet is responsible for making the individual flexible and multitalented, but also impatient. The natives also cherish a love for travel. Moreover, if aspected by Uranus, the native could become somewhat unconventional. The natives have agreeable faces, a translucent quality to the skin, eyes that attract attention and a tendency to be laid-back and relaxed.

This planet has an impact on the brain, the eyes and the bladder. Disorders of the stomach and the kidneys and those related to fertility are a result of this planet. It could easily be considered the ruler of life or Hyleg in a horoscope, since it frequently endows the native with a reasonably long lifespan.

It governs the metal silver. Its day is Monday. It can be interpreted to symbolise the mother or the wife.

As far as one's character is concerned, the natives have an agreeable disposition. However, they are in the habit of making mountains of molehills. Introvert, perceptive, creative and versatile, the natives have a great deal of patience and can bear unpleasant situations for a long time. However, they are very quick to change when they cross their limit of endurance. They also have immense ability to lie back and simply let the world pass them by.

Love Life

True romantics at heart, they tend to reminisce over the shared sweet moments and think about their beloved. Feelings and sentiments have a significant role to play in their lives. Moreover, these feelings have a profundity and intensity that can at times, have an adverse effect on their mental equilibrium. In times of solitude, they like to reflect and dwell upon romance. They hold on to all those things that bring rays of sunshine into their lives.

Reunions, festivals, parties and social gatherings on the whole, bring a great deal of happiness to them. They cherish bonds and relationships, especially with the family. For them, family is extremely important and they value it more than anything else. They place their life partners and children at the very centre of their universe, and life completely revolves around them. Nothing else can take the place of family for them. Such is the strength of their attachment to the family.

Although they remain relatively detached and do not poke their noses into the lives of others such as neighbours and friends, they are deeply involved in the lives of their family members, since for them they take prime importance.

Accepting and tolerant, they have an open heart and an ability to understand that their beloved would have both perfections and imperfections. And they show their understanding by never bringing up the imperfections. However, they also expect their partners to show them the same love, devotion and tolerance.

Finance and Profession

Though number 2 is a money making number, insecurity will always come their way. In particular cases, changeable conditions will also apply. There is likely to be a general feeling of uncertainty, giving way to a desire to take a jump at any chance to make money. In the end, this is likely to become a kind of vicious circle which is inclined to become worse as one gets older.

They should exercise extreme caution while dealing with financial matters. They should avoid speculation and all forms of gambling and should endeavour to build up their reserves, no matter how long it takes. All 'get rich quick' schemes should be avoided and if possible, they should become associated with or work for solid established businesses.

Their planetary conditions favour shipping, exports and transportation of goods or people, or the opening up of undeveloped countries.

Persons born on these dates have commercial careers. They may be sailors in navy, may be associated with import and export businesses and transport or travel. They also make good caterers, restaurant managers, orators, preachers, and contractors. They are also interested in developing vedic and sacred texts.

Health and Food

They are extremely sensitive to their surroundings; if these are favourable, they will probably get through life without much trouble. If, on the contrary, they are forced to live under depressing or unhappy conditions, they are liable to suffer a great deal from bodily troubles. In other words, it will be largely a question of the effect of 'the mind over matter.' There is a general tendency towards unaccountable pains and internal cramps in the internal organs. There is some likelihood of tumours, lesions and adhesions in connection with the intestines.

FAVOURABLE FOODS:
- Fish
- Potatoes
- Watermelons
- Melons
- Mushrooms

UNFAVOURABLE FOODS:
- Pastries, cakes and junk food

• Lucky Numbers • Days • Alphabets • Colours	
LUCKY NUMBERS AND DATES	2, 11, 20, 29, 38, 47, 7, 16, 61 70, 25, 34, 43,52
LUCKY DAY	Monday
LUCKY ALPHABETS	H, D, T
LUCKY COLOURS	White, light yellow, sea colour
LUCKY GEMS	Pearl or Cat's eye
LUCKY METALS	Silver, aluminium and platinum
LUCKY TALISMAN	A shoe in silver to be worn next to skin
LUCKY FLOWERS	White rose, jasmine

MANTRA
Aum shran shrin shron se: chandraye nameh

Number 3

Persons born on

3, 12, 21 or 30

3

Jupiter symbolises number 3. It is a planet that has many benefits and is highly positive. It stands for protection and is also referred to as the planet of fortune, since it enhances the prosperity of the native and helps to remove anything that is unfortunate from his life.

Jupiter is moderate, arid, yet productive; its colour is pale purplish blue; its metal is copper and Thursday is its day.

Its domicile is in Sagittarius; its night domicile in Pisces; its place of exaltation is in Cancer; its fall in Capricorn; it is in exile in Gemini and Virgo and its joy is in Sagittarius.

As far as placement is concerned, this planet is closest to the earth in Aries and farthest away in Libra.

Influential and dominating, this planet is responsible for creating diplomats, officials of religious bodies, government personnel and also exercises a lot of power over businessmen and others who are in the limelight.

Persons have energetic and happy temperaments. They are generous, yet can show a degree of self-centeredness in certain aspects. They also have a fondness for good food, parties and social gatherings. They are orderly and organised. They are close to their families, have a strong drive to achieve honour and name in society. However, this may at times be seen as a tendency towards pride and conceit.

The planet Jupiter tends to make the natives prone to blood disorders, gout and apoplexy. In short, disorders that are results of a rich and comfortable life.

Jupiter is a friend of the Moon and an opponent of Mars. This alliance has a role in indicating that the natives are moderately tall and strong built with slightly stooping shoulders. They have oval shaped faces and high, prominent foreheads. Premature balding and excessive sweating characterise the natives.

Love Life

It gives them a great deal of happiness when they and their partners find joy in the same things. These could be anything; from a poem, a common cause, or any activities. It is important that there is a strong feeling of sharing, oneness and togetherness. They want to feel that their partners are their soulmates. Individualism and isolation do not agree with them. Their passion and fervour are stoked by a strong bond with their partners. Moreover, they are of the opinion that it is essential that their partners and they have interests other than physical love to bind them and keep their relationship alive. What they look for is an ideal marriage—literally or figuratively. And it is not in their nature to settle for anything else. If they ever get the feeling that the two of them are drifting apart or lack a strong bond, they would be disappointed. Hence, they make it a point to keep the magic alive in their relationship and give it a kind of newness whenever they can. Emotional ties are stronger for them than mere physical ones.

Profession and Finance

They are good teachers, orators, bank employees and politicians. They are attached to religious and educational institutions too. Editing and publishing are rewarding. They can also be the heads of companies, lawyers, civil engineers, contractors, can be involved in foreign assignments. Speculation is risky.

Jupiter is their ruling planet; they may certainly expect good fortune and a generous slice of luck in money matters. They are sure to accumulate wealth in whatever work they are engaged in, but are inclined to take risks and at times, lose heavily by speculation. They never blame others for their losses and rather fall back on their work or profession and build up their bank balance again.

Health and Food

Generally such persons have splendid physical constitution and suffer very little from illnesses of any kind, upto the age of about sixty. However, after sixty, there is a change generally, and if they do not lessen their responsibilities, the nervous system will begin to break down bringing on some form of paralysis affecting the spine, arms, hands and the brain. They should avoid over-work and focus on complete rest and spiritualism.

FAVOURABLE FOODS:
- Raw eggs
- Raw vegetables
- Fruits
- Tomatoes
- Beans
- Corn

UNFAVOURABLE FOODS:
- Spicy food and smoking

• Lucky Numbers • Days • Alphabets • Colours	
LUCKY NUMBERS AND DATES	All the series of 3 3, 12, 21, 30
LUCKY DAY	Thursday .
LUCKY ALPHABETS	Y, Dh, F, Ph, Bh, Gh
LUCKY COLOURS	Yellow, off-white, orange
LUCKY GEM	Pukhraj
LUCKY METAL	Gold
LUCKY TALISMAN	A gold anchor to be worn next to skin
LUCKY FLOWERS	Sunflower, rose, pink rose
LUCKY PERFUME	Lign-aloes
DAY OF FAST	Thursday

MANTRA
Aum gran grien gron sai: gurvey nameh

Number 4

Persons born on
4, 13 or 22

4

The planet Uranus is symbolic of Number 4. Uranus, along with Neptune, is considered a transcendental planet. It seems that the planet borrows certain traits and attributes from Saturn, Mars and Jupiter. Its colour is a deep blue. Its domicile is in Aquarius; its exile in Leo; its exaltation in Scorpio and its fall in Taurus.

The planet is quite distinct. It is cold, arid, intellectual, anxious and variable. There is a strong effect of this planet on the nerves and the brain of the native.

Depending upon the position that it holds in the house and sign, this planet is responsible for bringing about unusual and uncharacteristic behaviour and events in the life of the natives.

The planet is a definite indicator of self-reliance and rebellion. However, it also happens to radiate a certain kind of unique brilliance. This brilliance may not be acknowledged early in the natives' lives, though it would bring them fame at some stage. Till that time, others could well consider them unconventional.

Uranus is considered an electro-magnetic planet and has a strong consequence on nations and collections of people, and can cause unforeseen and disastrous occurences. Since the planet borrows from Saturn and Mars and is also influenced by Jupiter, it has a more serious impact on the occurences that take place.

When the cards are laid out, Uranus indicates a dominant and unprecedented occurence that could take place depending upon the aspects received as well as the house and sign. On the whole though, this planet represents problems in the family, innovativeness yet peculiarity as well as a self-centered attitude.

Love Life

They have a somewhat austere approach to love and romance. What they want is simple. Their partners should love them and at the same time, not infringe upon their personal space. Since they have an individualistic streak, they often want to be left to their own thoughts and ideas. This is when they want their partners to be understanding.

Creative and imaginative, they think of unusual ways to romance their loved ones and give them a feeling of being the most special and privileged. However, it is important that they do not hold the same expectations from their partners. They need to curb their egoistic tendencies and be more giving in their relationships. Otherwise, chances are that they could end up quite disappointed. Their spontaneity will ensure that there is never a dull moment. They constantly think of ways to enliven and enhance their romantic escapades. They enjoy the feeling of being the centre of someone's existence. The warmth of love is something that they tend to value. However, their unusual temperament may sometimes send off the wrong signals. Therefore, they must ensure that they keep the passion alive in the relationship.

Determined and willful, they can be quite demanding in love. While they want their space, they can be quite possessive of their partners. They demand complete loyalty and fidelity, and if at any time, they feel that they are not getting that, they walk out easily without as much as a backward glance. This should not imply that they are insensitive. In fact, they are quite tender-hearted. It is just that they are practical and prudent in matters of the heart as well.

As long as they give as much as they take, they will enjoy a fruitful and blissful relationship. It is essential that they let their partners be and give them the same space that they require. They must spend time together, share and build happy memories, without imposing on each other. They should let their partners get used to their quirks and oddities. And at the same time, adjust to the temperament of their mates. Given their tenderness and humane disposition, there is no reason why they will not have successful relationships.

Profession and Finance

Persons born on these dates can always make money, provided they apply themselves to that purpose. They are however liable to lose money by actions caused by their opposite sex or by litigation and by blackmail.

Politics fascinate them. They are usually involved in things related to sports, automobiles, medical discoveries, and may be authors, astronauts, alcoholics and pianists.

Health and Food

Such persons have the appearance of being more healthy than they really are. They get little or no warning about illnesses, they often suddenly collapse from heart failure or a clot of blood in the brain.

FAVOURABLE FOODS:
- Fish
- Pear
- Lemon
- Oranges
- Radish
- Grapes
- Peach

• Lucky Numbers • Days • Alphabets • Colours	
LUCKY NUMBERS AND DATES	8, 17, 26, 35, 44, 53, 62
LUCKY DAY	Saturday
LUCKY ALPHABETS	L, A, Ch
LUCKY COLOURS	Black, grey, dark brown, dark blue
LUCKY GEMS	Neelam and all kinds of dark sapphire
LUCKY METALS	Iron steel and aluminium
LUCKY TALISMAN	A horse shoe
LUCKY FLOWERS	Ivy and pansies
LUCKY PERFUME	Galbanum
DAY OF FAST	Saturday

MANTRA
Aum aein hrin sri: shancharye nameh

Number 5

Persons born on

5, 14 or 23

5

Mercury is the planet that governs number 5. Highly changeable, the planet affects the mind. It also exerts significant influence, since it is deeply impacted by the aspects which it receives, as well as the opposing aspects. Its day house is in Gemini; night house in Virgo; its exile is in Sagittarius and exaltation is in Pisces. The planet is beneficial for all elements related to learning and education. In fact, this planet is taken into special consideration when forming an assessment of the native's mental state.

Mercury has a significant effect on fields of commerce, medicine, language, composing, etc. Since it is realistic; we find that it influences the individual's fortune, wealth, and real estate. Quicksilver is the metal governed by Mercury. Vigour, vivacity, energy and activity are all represented by this planet. When it is adversely influenced, it governs traits like lying, cheating, deceit and deception.

Its colour is light grey and its day is Wednesday.

The natives are bestowed with several distinctive characteristics. It makes them good humoured and quick at repartee. They have investigative and logical minds, are gifted with lean, beautiful hands which they often use to make a point in discussions. The height is average to short, and the body has athletic flexibility. The nose is thin and somewhat long while the forehead is high.

Disorders of the nervous system are caused by the dominance of Mercury. While the natives have mental agility, they may not always behave with a lot of dignity. Since they do not like to be challenged and opposed, they are rigid when it comes to professional interactions and to a degree, even personal relationships. People under this planet are often at odds with the rest of the society due to their unconventional approach and frequently take the path less walked. When favourably aspected, this planet is beneficial for professionals in the fields of law and creative writing.

Love Life

Number 5 is noted for the single status of its natives. While this does not imply that they do not have any romantic inclinations, it does imply that they do not plunge headlong into a relationship. They watch and wait till they are absolutely sure of their feelings and only then put their faith in someone. They tend to view their feelings and emotions with their head and hence, are wary of what love will bring. Moreover, they draw inferences from the relationships and marriages they see around them to form the basis of their own relationships. Therefore, it is quite possible, that their overly judgmental attitude could hamper their happiness and contentment. It is essential that they avoid being too analytical and savour the moment. It would go a long way in solidifying their relationships with their partners. They should cherish the feelings of being in love and the colour of romance. Being born under number 5 does signify that they use their heads than their hearts. It does not imply that they are completely detached and distant. It is just that they wish to establish the essence of emotions before they decide to believe in them, and let them guide their actions.

Finance and Profession

This is a difficult number to interpret. In matters of finance, the natives' quick-witted clever brains will give them great opportunities. At times they are likely to be very rich and at other times the very reverse. They should adapt themselves to the lowest sphere. In fact, the greatest danger is that they are, by nature, adaptable to others as well as to different conditions.

If they make the effort to hold their nature in check, they would easily become successful in whatever enterprise, industry, or work they are associated with. This is a remarkably good combination for all who have to deal with people.

Such persons are interested in varied jobs as they are active, alert and industrious. Being good speakers, intelligent and humorous, they are fit for politics. Other suitable professions are brokers, share market agents, businessmen, secretaries, scientists and advocates. They may be journalists, travelling agents and have jobs connected with these.

Health and Food

Health wise, they are inclined to be their worst enemies. They have an excellent constitution, but of the highly strung type. They take too much out of themselves in every possible way. They prone to live on their nerves and crave for change and travel. In order to 'keep going', they are at times liable to indulge in stimulants which harm their digestive organs. As they desist rules and regulations, they are not inclined to be regular in their habits, but may eat at any time of the day and night, and only sleep as and when they can.

Hence, they are likely to harm the splendid constitution they would otherwise have. They are liable to have trouble brought on by the nerves, twitching of the eyelids, some defect in the tongue that affects speech, blood disorders, eczema and skin eruptions. They should not nibble their food, eat regularly and learn to relax.

FAVOURABLE FOODS:
- Red meat
- Fish
- Egg
- Plums
- Oranges
- Water

UNFAVOURABLE HABITS:
- Smoking

Lucky Numbers • Days • Alphabets • Colours	
LUCKY NUMBERS AND DATES	All series of 5 ie, 5, 14, 23,32, 41,50
LUCKY DAY	Wednesday
LUCKY ALPHABETS	K, Gh, Chh, H
LUCKY COLOUR	Green
LUCKY METALS	Silver, gold
LUCKY TALISMAN	An engraved figure 5 in gold to be worn next to the skin
LUCKY FLOWERS	Balm, celery, lavender, brylonia

MANTRA

Aum bran brin bron se: budhaye nameh

Number 6

Persons born on

6, 15 or 24

6

Number 6 corresponds to the planet Venus. Venus has many appealing attributes. It is known to be pleasant, moist, interesting productive and compassionate. Its day domicile is in Libra. Its night domicile is in Taurus and its fall in Virgo.

The planet has a fortifying effect and is frequently referred to as the 'lesser fortune'. This is a planet that signifies beautiful things, and emotions of love and passion.

When the cards are laid out, the planet symbolises the female form.

Venus symbolises warmth, friendliness, relationships and a fondness for music, poetry, etc. It bestows the individual with several favourable attributes. The natives are generous, loving, tender, and happy, and enjoy the comforts of life. Temperamentally, the planet can, in a few cases, make them egocentric. As far as looks are concerned, they have elegant features and well-formed faces.

The inherent elegance and grace in the natives, due to the influence of Venus, brings about subtle sensuality. This, if not influenced adversely, would be as sophisticated and understated as the planet itself.

The planet also makes the natives extravagant. They enjoy splurging on luxuries for their pleasure and also for others. They do not settle for anything but the best, whether it is clothes, shoes, or even friends. Although they are helpful and caring and have a wide circle of friends and associates, they wish to associate with people who hold an exalted position in society.

The native may be prone to disorders of the chest and generative system due to the lifestyle choices.

When placed in the chart of a woman, the planet is not very beneficial as far as marriage is concerned, since it indicates a husband who could be a gambler, womaniser or one who has some other bad habits.

Love Life

The emotion of love is as innate as emotions of anger, joy and hurt. They have passionate and intense sensuality which translates into a deep respect for love and affection. Romance is not treated lightly by them. In fact, they give it a lot of weight in their daily lives. As a result, this beautiful emotion has a lot of importance for them.

Since love and romance have a significant place in their lives, they tend to worship their beloved and hence, may even be somewhat controlling and overprotective. Valuable and cherished, these are the feelings that they associate with their beloved. Just as they would make their partners feel most important, they want to experience the same emotional and mental security. They want to be sure that their partners love them completely and implicitly. That, for them, is the most beautiful aspect of being in love and loving someone.

While love is something they give a lot of importance to, they are quite wary of marrying someone in a hurry. It is important that they be completely sure about the loyalty and devotion of their partners. The two of them should have the same set of values as far as home, family and children are concerned. Marriage is a serious affair for them and they want to give it their one hundred per cent.

More than anything, they need to be convinced about the sincerity of their beloveds' love. Anything which seems superficial to them will not meet with their approval. In fact, they have the ability to see through any kind of façade. Hence, love and romance occupy an exalted place in their lives.

Finance and Profession

They are fortunate in investments and in matters of finance generally, especially if they follow their own intuition. They are lucky in partnership or in business investments and in matters dealing with the public. They are restless and keep shifting and can face problems in finding the right profession where they can make money. They should be firm and positive and ready to say 'no'.

They may be government servants or officers. They lead a social life. They are best suited for law, and make good chemists, electric engineers and painters. They may deal with articles of feminine interests and luxury or amusement. They may also be writers, musicians, singers and actors. They may have professions related to the navy or transport.

Health and Food

On account of their having great recuperative powers, they are not likely to suffer from many illnesses with the exception of the danger of tumours. In early years, they are likely to have inflamed tonsils and some trouble at the back of the tongue and throat. The kidney, the back, the buttocks and the generative organs are weak health zones. The nervous system is sensitive. A disturbing environment could result in upsetting their health.

FAVOURABLE FOODS:
- Brown rice
- Peas
- Wheat
- Milk
- Strawberries
- Spinach
- Corn

UNFAVOURABLE FOODS:
- Sugar and starch

• Lucky Numbers • Days • Alphabets • Colours	
LUCKY NUMBERS AND DATES	All series of 6 ie, 6, 15, 24, 42, 51, 60
LUCKY DAY	Friday
LUCKY ALPHABETS	R, T
LUCKY COLOURS	Blue, royal blue
LUCKY GEMS	Diamond or sapphire
LUCKY METALS	Silver, platinum and aluminum
LUCKY TALISMAN	A scale, key or shoe made of silver and platinum to be worn next to the skin.
LUCKY FLOWERS	Lily, white rose and kali

MANTRA
Aum hran hrin hron sei: shukraye nameh

Number 7

Persons born on

7 16 or 25

7

Neptune is the planet that governs and symbolises number 7. As per analyses and observations, this planet is closely related to Venus and the Moon. Its characteristics are quite similar to these planets. Neptune is mild, moist and has closeness for Pisces. Pisces may be its domicile. Its exile appears to be in Virgo, its exaltation in Cancer and its joy in Capricorn.

From what can be made out, this planet has an impact on the nation and the world in general, rather than on specific people. Hence, it tends to be more powerful in its effects over countries rather than a single individual. When reading a horoscope, the presence of this planet can be translated into influencing events which may be caused in conjunction with the presence of other planets as well.

The planet is favourable for undertaking journeys and the pursuit of an interest in occult practices or related topics. Neptune has the tendency to bestow the individual with certain unique traits. It makes the native sentimental and his mind is nervous and anxious. Fickleness is another trait that results due to the presence of this planet. Wealth, money and legacies are also linked to the presence of Neptune. And if it is favourably aspected, it can bring good fortune for the individual as well. On the other hand, the planet is not positive as far as marriage and relationships are concerned. It can result in arguments and conflicts in a marriage.

General weakness and lymphatic disorders are ruled by Neptune, depending upon the sign in which it is placed. For example, in Capricorn, it will signify weakness of the knees; in Pisces, gout and rheumatism in the feet.

This planet has a marked influence over the feelings and sentiments of the natives. In other words, Neptune dominates the heart more than the head and hence, emotions precede their reason and logic.

Love Life

Love has a higher dimension for them. They connect better on a spiritual plane and hence their thoughts and views regarding love have a deeper meaning. Love is not selfish. The want to use it to improve life and the world. So much so, that they could even let their personal love lives take a backseat due to preoccupation with causes that require greater involvement from them. While they should continue to spread love throughout the world, they should not forget to make it an integral part of their personal lives. This is what helps them to evolve and grow as an individual.

Bringing happiness to the lives of their partners is what gives them great joy. Sacrificing and giving, they let their own interests take a backseat in the face of the happiness and contentment of those they cherish. They are extremely affectionate, warm and kind. All that they desire is to give warmth to everybody they meet or interact with.

So important is the presence of love and romance in their lives that when they experience true love, it brings out their best qualities. They pour in all efforts to make their home a haven of happiness. Words of caution though; they should spend sufficient time in selecting the right partners for themselves. It is important that their partners are on the same mental level.

If they are cheated in love and are married to people who are cruel and self-centered, they would be extremely miserable and disappointed. Therefore, it is important that they do not let themselves be manipulated. They should trust their instincts and intellect when finding the right partners and making a decision about marriage. A happy marriage would definitely bring out the best in them.

Finance and Profession

They are ambitious and out to make money, but are very careful of their name and reputation. They will gain by solid enterprise and have every likelihood of becoming wealthy. They show an enterprising spirit in all their undertakings and will rise to prominence in whatever career they choose.

They can be successful accountants, bankers, musicians, opera house singers and actors. They make good businessmen and can be good liaison officers, managing directors and organisers. They will succeed in the navy or shipping corporations and in the field of occult science. They may deal in drinks, beverages, cosmetics, chemicals, and may be involved in medical and educational departments.

Health and Food

This question largely depends on their outlook on life. As long as they continue to be active, they will keep well and healthy. If forced for any reason into inactivity, they become pleasure-loving and indolent, inclined to put on weight and let the reins of life easily drop from their hands.

FAVOURABLE FOODS:
- Egg yolks
- Onions
- Grains
- Lamb
- Pears

• Lucky Numbers • Days • Alphabets • Colours	
LUCKY NUMBERS AND DATES	3, 12, 21, 30
LUCKY DAY	Thursday
LUCKY ALPHABETS	H, D, C
LUCKY COLOUR	Yellow
LUCKY GEMS	Pukhraj and topaz
LUCKY METAL	Gold
LUCKY TALISMAN	A couple of fishes
LUCKY FLOWER	Marigold

MANTRA

Aum gran grin gron sri guravey nameh

Number 8

Persons born on
8, 17 or 26

The planet Saturn symbolises number 8. This planet is a cold, dry and barren planet; its dry domicile is in Aquarius; its nocturnal domicile in Capricorn. Saturn is exiled in Leo and in Cancer. Its exaltation is at 21 degrees of Libra; its joy in Capricorn. Its fall is in Aries. It is farthest from the earth in Sagittarius and closest to it in Gemini.

The planet has a strong impact on the bone structure and the digestive system. The natives are tall with brown or black hair and their skin has a slightly sallow tinge to it.

Lead is the metal for Saturn and dark green is its colour. Its day is Saturday.

As far as attitude is concerned, the natives have cynical and suspicious temperaments. Although they might lack in confidence, they are conceited. Hardworking and diligent, they careful in all that they do and have a serious outlook towards life.

The planet is an intelligent planet and ensures that the natives have an extremely logical mind which can somehow inhibit the natives and prevent them from taking a liberal approach. This planet is responsible for making scientists, engineers and researchers.

This planet is called the 'great misfortune'. If it is badly situated in a horoscope, its adverse effects on the houses or other planets can be quite fatal. However, despite the title, when the planet is situated in powerful places, it can be responsible for rewarding the natives with fortune and fame.

Although the planet is responsible for delaying and postponing events, however, in its own way, it stands for steadiness and security, as long as its aspects are favourable.

Landed wealth and assets are influenced by Saturn.

While the natives are gifted with long life, they will have to endure many continual illnesses and ailments.

When the cards are laid out, they symbolise conceit, capable advice, longevity and endurance.

Love Life

Fundamentally, the natives want to get the love and affection of their lovers. Only then would they want to share their love with their partners. Respect and their sense of confidence are critical for them. This is a somewhat selfish attitude and there could be a time when their partners could become offended and end a possibly meaningful relationship with suddenness.

Love, romance and affection are extremely important for them, and marriage gives them an elevated sense of happiness and contentment. However, their expectations of their partners are rather high. They want their partners to be good-looking and will not settle for anything but the best. As a matter of fact, they can even be quite critical too.

Considering that they have high aspirations, they find that their emotions and ambitions are often in conflict. It is important that they are not too controlling and overwhelming, since that can easily end their hopes of a loving and caring relationship. No partner would want to be with someone who is overly critical and dominating.

When married, they want their partners to give them happiness, respect and space; however, they often overlook the needs of their partners. Moreover, they insist on their opinions and views, resulting in some amount of disagreements. They need partners who love them immensely in order to be patient with them. Yet they have such an appeal that they are capable wining anyone over with their magnetism. Still, it would help them to be more appreciative and giving.

Finance and Profession

In spite of great opportunities, they are not likely to make much provision for failing years. Although capable of giving splendid advice to others, they do not follow it themselves. To the surprise of their friends, towards the end of their days, they are likely to become comparatively poor having given their money away to others or making peculiar provisions in their wills. They need to exercise great prudence and care if they are to keep their position and wealth.

They may be contractors, cement brokers, dealers in scientific instruments, physicians and will gain through lands, mines, kerosene or petrol and chemicals.

Health and Food

Sudden and unexpected illness is likely. Stoppages and strictures of the internal organs and operations may be expected, but against that, there will be long periods of good health. They should study all questions of diet with more care than the average person, and not allow themselves to live for any length of time in damp low-lying places.

They are liable to have injuries of the lower limbs, weakness or turning of the ankles and injuries of the spinal column caused by falls or by accidents. Though the Saturnine influence indicates good physical stamina, but their tendency towards depression causes complicated health problems. They should be optimistic and cheerful in order to remain healthy.

FAVOURABLE FOODS:
- Figs
- Green vegetables
- Cow's milk
- Oranges
- Lemons
- Egg yolk
- Cheese
- Fish
- Food grains

• Lucky Numbers • Days • Alphabets • Colours	
LUCKY NUMBERS AND DATES	8, 17, 26, 25, 44, 53, 62
LUCKY DAY	Saturday
LUCKY ALPHABETS	G, J, Kh, Bh
LUCKY COLOURS	Black, grey, dark brown or blue
LUCKY GEMS	Neelam and all varieties of dark sapphire
LUCKY METALS	Iron, steel and aluminium
LUCKY TALISMAN	A horse shoe
LUCKY FLOWERS	Ivy and pansies

MANTRA
Aum aien hrin sri: shancharye nameh

Number 9

Persons born on

9, 18 or 27

9

Number 9 is represented by Mars which is a dry, hot and masculine planet. Its day domicile is in Aries, and its night domicile in Scorpio. It is in exile in the domiciles of Venus, Taurus and Libra; its exaltation is in Capricorn, its fall in the opposite sign Cancer, and it receives joy in Scorpio.

It is farthest from the Earth when situated in Virgo, and is, on the contrary, nearest when in Pisces.

The planet endows the natives with spontaneity, intensity, enthusiasm, and energy.

The physical characteristics of a number 9 person are an average built, but good health. The muscles are robust, since they are the body parts ruled by the planet. The native has the ability to fight off infections and illnesses. The face and the body have certain sense of authority and recklessness. The hair is usually brown in colour and somewhat thin.

The planet represents men who attract women on the basis of their physical strength and ability. On the flip side, they do not gain a lot of favour among men and are known to pick fights and arguments. When influenced in a beneficial manner, they are gifted with gracious and superior characteristics. They do not hesitate to stand up for those who are weaker than them and shield them bravely.

The influence of Mars leads to the natives having a preference for sports. Since the natives have strong constitution and a liking for combat, they make good soldiers. However, the native, also do well in other fields, since they have a dependable and positive attitude to life.

Its colour is bright red; metal is iron and day is Tuesday. It is responsible for causing fever, inflammatory disorders and accidents or injuries.

Love Life

The phenomenon of romance holds a lot of significance. It rules their thought processes and they are preoccupied with the notions of being in love with someone or the other. Every single action of theirs and all their views would, in one way or the other, be connected to love and romance. They are suffused with the beautiful flush of romance and their emotions are passionate and intense.

Although they may be highly self-reliant, yet when in love with someone, they are surprisingly dependent and mellow. They get happiness listening to their partners and also doing whatever they want. As a matter of fact, they could even be somewhat passive. However, not many people want to point out this fact, since they do not take criticism easily or positively on this sensitive and extremely personal issue.

Considering that they fall in love easily and quickly, they should ensure that they do not get married in a rush. They are drawn towards a number of people; hence, it is wiser that they exercise caution. People are drawn to them as well, since they are vivacious and attractive. Therefore, they should take their time and will definitely meet someone who would meet their ideals and respect, and will love them implicitly.

Consistent yet romantic, they are able to discover the secrets a lasting and blissful love life. They are truly ideal examples of eternal love.

Finance and Profession

The natives are involved in professions related to chemistry, medicine, insurance and the maternity department. They are involved in research work, iron and steel works, the military and naval departments. They can be good politicians, orators and composers of great musical works, actors, dramatists and CID detectives too.

As a rule, they are successful in whatever they undertake after a hard uphill fight in their early years; but they may expect to overcome all obstacles and difficulties and gain money and prestige.

They are hard workers and their sense of purpose in life makes them serious about making money. They have an excellent business sense and generally handle high financial matters. Their scope is wide and varies from physicians, chemists, detectives, to spiritualists, military leaders. They make excellent hypnotists and surgeons.

Health and Food

They have a strong constitution with phenomenal stamina. They are usually short of breath though. They are prone to fevers of all kinds and high blood pressure and heart problems. They meet with accidents, chiefly those caused by machines, and fire arms. They are prone to accidents and likely to meet violent mobs. The sex organs, throat, and tonsils are sensitive health zones. Drugs and alcohol should be avoided at all costs. Health seeking habits should be given importance. their cell salt, calcium sulphate is to be used in the repair of tissues. They should make it a point to include onions, greens and cauliflowers and cereals in their diet.

FAVOURABLE FOODS:
- Onions
- Mustard
- Cabbages
- Fish
- Honey
- Radish
- Coconut

• Lucky Numbers • Days • Alphabets • Colours	
LUCKY NUMBERS AND DATES	1,10,19,28.37,46,55, 4,13,22, 31, 40, 49
LUCKY DAY	Sunday
LUCKY ALPHABETS	M, T
LUCKY COLOURS	Red, orange and white
LUCKY GEMS	Ruby or amber
LUCKY TALISMAN	A sun in gold to be worn next to the skin
LUCKY FLOWERS	Red rose, sunflower, rosemary

MANTRA
Aum hran hrin hron sai suryaye nameh

Numbers and Their Significance

Numbers and Sun Signs

NUMBERS	SUN SIGNS
1	Leo
2	Cancer
3	Sagittarius
4	Aquarius
5	Gemini and Virgo
6	Taurus and Libra
7	Pisces
8	Capricorn
9	Scorpio

Numbers and Elements

NUMBER	ELEMENT
1	Fire
2	Water
3	Fire
4	Air
5	Air
6	Earth
7	Water
8	Earth
9	Fire

Numbers and Body Parts

1	Head
2	Heart, chest and lungs
3	Thighs and feet
4	Ankle and toes
5	Neck, hands, ears and breath
6	Face, eyes and nose
7	Fingers and nails
8	Blood
9	Hair and sexual organs

Numbers and Directions

1	East
2	Northeast
3	Northeast
4	East
5	North
6	Southeast
7	Northeast
8	West
9	South

Numbers and Stones

NUMBERS	STONES
1	Ruby
2	Pearl
3	Pukhraj
4	Gomed

5	Emerald
6	Diamond
7	Cat's eye
8	Blue sapphire
9	Moonga

Numbers and Days

NUMBERS	DAY
1	Sunday
2	Monday
3	Thursday
4	Saturday
5	Wednesday
6	Friday
7	Thursday
8	Saturday
9	Tuesday

Numbers and Favourable Countries

NUMBERS	COUNTRIES
1	India, Pakistan, Turkey, Burma, Afghanistan, Japan
2	London, Tibet, France, Germany, Sri Lanka, Delhi, Kabul, Ethopia
3	England, Nepal, Cambodia, Holland, Australia, USA, Denmark, Bhutan
4	Italy, UAE, India, Hungry

5	Korea, Saudi Arabia, Singapore, Spain, America,
6	Canada, Russia, Czechoslovakia, Japan, New Zealand
7	Russia, Thailand, Sweden, Scotland
8	China, Malaysia, Austria
9	Indonesia, India, Persia

Numbers and Favourable Months

NUMBERS	MONTHS
1	January, March, May, July, September, October, December
2	April, September, November
3	March, May, July, September, October, December
4	February, April, June, August, September, November
5	January, March, May, July, August, October, December
6	February, April, June, November
7.	January, March, May, August, September, October
8.	January, March, April, May, July, August, December
9.	February, March, April, June, July, September, November, December

Numbers and Professions

NUMBER 1

They are involved in electronics and are designers, jewellers, promotors, forest officers, commission agents.

NUMBER 2

They are involved in diary products, paper, hotel and restaurant, navy, docks, chemicals, dancing, acting, sea products and are antique dealers.

NUMBER 3

They are involved in teaching, social service, are diplomats, lawyers, judges, secretaries, bankers, brokers, salesmen, policemen and part of the tourism industry.

NUMBER 4

They are pilots technicians, engineers, architects, magicians, lecturers, fashion designers, lecturers, government servants and are involved in railways.

NUMBER 5

They are engineers, salesmen, accountants, lawyers, writers, journalists, insurance agents, publishers and book sellers

NUMBER 6

They are vaastu experts, jewellers, restaurant owners, designers, musicians, social workers, writers, dealers and painters.

NUMBER 7

They are swimmers, actors, film producers, detectives, sellers of liquid items, editors, magicians and involved in professions related to the navy and dairy products.

NUMBER 8

They are sports persons, engineers, policemen, army personal, contractors, forest officers, coal merchants and medical representatives.

NUMBER 9

They are doctors, bankers, lawyers, chemists, mechanical engineers, preachers, writers and administrators.

Numbers—Friends and Enemies

NUMBER	FRIENDS	ENEMIES	NEUTRAL
1	2, 7, 5	6, 8	3, 4, 9
2	5, 6, 3, 8	7, 8	1, 4
3	2, 7, 6, 8	5, 6	1, 4
4	2, 5, 7	1, 6, 8	3, 9
5	1, 3, 4	8, 9	2, 7
6	3	9	1, 2, 5, 5, 7
7	3, 5, 6, 8	2, 9	1, 4
8	3	1, 4	2, 5, 6, 7, 9
9	8	5, 6	1, 2, 3, 4, 7

Numbers and Days

Born on Sunday

Persons born on Sunday are ruled by the Sun. This planet is dry, warm and positive. It is somewhat barren, but is favourable towards commercial undertakings and money matters. It procures the support of influential people. In a layout of the cards, it is taken for the Day as it brings light, success, stability and fixity in all things.

The day governs the metals, gold and copper.

Persons born on 1, 10, 19 or 28 of any month or whose sun sign is Leo, are influenced by this day.

The Sun also represents Apollo, the god of light, with his harmoniously formed body, captivating beauty, his gaze lost in infinity, the one who meditates serenely about dreams of power.

This tarot card represents the father. It promises enlightenment for everything it approaches. It is an indication of stability, power, strength, ambition and success. It brings gold and compels the earning or spending of money. It depicts children at play which means that a new day is dawning. The air is fresh, the sky is blue and all is well. In symbolic terms; a life without the sun would be a life in total darkness. There will be growth and happiness if one seeks the blessings of a father or an elder brother.

People who are facing unhappiness and emptiness, or whose minds are unclear, must wear red or orange.

ARTICLES FOR DONATION:		Wheat, copper, red cloth, flowers, sandalwood
BEEJ MANTRA	:	*Aum hram hreem hraum se suraye nameh*
YOUR DEITY	:	Fire and Lord Rudra
DIRECTION	:	East
LUCKY STONE	:	A ruby of 5 carats to be worn on Sunday before 8.00 am after Pran Pratishtha.

The shastras say that any person who recites the above mantra 7000 times in thirty days can be enriched by past experiences of his life. He may begin a new stage in life on a higher plane; wiser and more confident. *Surya namaskar* and the offering of water to the rising sun can definitely bring hope and promise. Optimism is the word of Sunday.

Born on Monday

Persons born on Monday are ruled by the Moon. This planet is feminine, cardinal, cold, nocturnal and belongs to the watery elements. It represents inconstancy. The card represents the mother, the wife, and is the guide of good fortune. The moon is the symbol of strong imagination and poetry, that inclines towards dreaminess, melancholy and sadness on full moon (pooranmashi) day.

Persons born on 2, 11, 20 or 29 of any month or whose sun sign is Cancer or Pisces are influenced by this day. When birth takes place between noon and midnight, life will be usually be a long one. It makes the natives changeable and versatile, restless and fond of travel, specially if born in the months of May or October. The moon represents the goddess of the night and the queen of silence. The indicates the oval shaped face of a woman with abundant fair hair and greyish blue eyes filled with gentle love and affection.

Persons born on Monday govern the metal silver. They can experience unexpected gains and great strokes of luck by donation and reciting the beej mantra of the moon.

ARTICLES FOR DONATION : Rice, milk, sugar, silver, white cloth
BEEJ MANTRA : *Om shraam shrim sharum cechandraye nameh*

YOUR DEITY : Durga and Parvati

DIRECTION : Northwest

LUCKY STONE : Pearl moonstone to be worn on Monday morning before 8.00 am after Pran Pratishtha.

The moon suggests that with just a little extra determination, they will be able to transform almost any area of their lives. The shastras mention that any person who recites the above mantra 11,000 times in thirty days, can experience moral and physical courage and success without much exertion. Memory and miracle are the words of Monday.

Monday is the day of Lord Shiva. Lord Shiva is the creator, preserver and the destroyer. He is the form of absolute truth which is of the nature of pure consciousness. He is worshipped in his phallic form, the lingam.

Any person suffering from emotional upheavals, educational phobia, underhand enmity, domestic disharmony or facing obstacles in foreign settlements, must worship Lord Shiva on Monday and go on a fast on this day.

Born on Tuesday

Persons born on Tuesday are ruled by the planet Mars. This planet is dry, hot and masculine. This planet exerts impetuosity, passion, energy, expansion and produces active temperament over those it rules. The tarot card represents a helmeted man, pike in hand and shield by his side, with his firm chin covered with a red beard. Mars, the god of war and passion is about to give in to the indulgence of love. It denotes health and physical resistance. It indicates anger and vitality. It is triumph of force; it denotes straightforwardness and represents the man.

Persons born on 9, 18, 27 of any month or whose sun sign is Aries and Scorpio, are much influenced by this day. The stature of the person is average, but generally has a robust constitution and strong muscles. It also gives the power of resistance. Generally, people tend to undertake bigger tasks than they are able to accomplish.

Mars represents the lover. It denotes anger, frankness, passion and strength. It brings success through industry and activity, and also through personal merit.

Persons born on Tuesday govern the metal copper. They are inclined towards sports and make aviators; they always make good soldiers in the time of war; but are strong-headed in times of peace.

Men may experience blood disorders and women may go through surgical treatment.

ARTICLES FOR DONATION :	Copper, wheat, ghee, masoor dal, red cloth.
BEEJ MANTRA :	*Om kraam kreem kraum se bhomayeh nameh*
YOUR DEITY :	Ganpati, Hanuman
DIRECTION :	South
LUCKY STONE :	Red coral to be worn on Tuesday evening after sunset, after Pran Pratishtha.

Tuesday is the day of Hanuman. The deity of war and celibacy (brahmcharya). Mars shows preservation and protection at the most critical moments. People born on this day are fond of luxuries and are spendthrift. Mars always indicates difficulty regarding marriage or a delayed union, which will eventually succeed. The shastras say that any person who recites the beej mantra 10,000 times in twenty days, can experience success, good friendship and daring will power, which will bring about freedom and the triumph of a happy marriage.

Born on Wednesday

Persons born on Wednesday are ruled by Mercury. This planet is mental, dry, nervous and convertible, that is to say, it is strongly modified both by the aspects which it receives, and by its position.

It is good for things connected with knowledge, and deserve special attention in order to judge the native's mentality.

It has special influence on commerce, medicine, speech, writing and letters. It also represents practical things and is connected with personal property and consequently with money.

Mercury also symbolises youth, liveliness, gaiety, motion, dancing, walking and represents the child. Its day is Wednesday. Quick silver is the metal governed by Mercury. Its colour is green and light grey.

The card represents two pretty little cherubins harmoniously united in their charming duality. It indicates refined taste, interest the arts, love of music, little constancy in the affections and success in business pursuits. The card also represents activity and power, as well as beauty. It stands for leaders of big undertakings with whom everything succeeds in the material sense. It brings about enlightenment, good reasoning powers and moral purity.

Persons born on 5, 14 or 23 of any month or whose sun sign is Gemini or Virgo are much influenced by this day.

Women born on Wednesday with ascendant mercury on Gemini are tender in expressing their feminity, having fairy-like tresses, she represents the kiss of love, and is idealistic and supreme, full of charm and grace.

ARTICLES FOR DONATION :	Sugar, green cloth, moong, camphor, turpentine oil
BEEJ MANTRA :	*Om bram breem braum se budhaye nameh*
YOUR DEITY :	Vishnu, Lord Naryana
DIRECTION :	North
LUCKY STONE :	Emerald to be worn on Wednesday morning after Pran Pratishtha.

The shastras mention that any person who recites the above mantra 19,000 times in twenty-one days, will be fortunate in love affairs and marriage. The success will ensue through courage and help. However, imagination, vision, shyness and preservence are the virtues of persons born on Wednesday.

Born on Thursday

Persons born on Thursday are ruled by Jupiter. This planet is temperate, dry and fruitful. Persons born on Thursday are lively, cheerful and benevolent. The native has a great sense of originality and administration; has love for his family and regard for respectability and esteem. But he also has a certain amount of vanity and a desire to patronise, with a view to self advertisement.

The card represents the Majestic with flowing hair, and Olympian beard, seated upon a throne of ivory, holding the lightning and the sacred eagle at his feet. Zeus, monarch and the father of the gods and of men, acquits himself of his duties and presides over the evolution of world and of nations, protecting the innocent, and chastising the wicked. This card represents the family, and material comforts. The native is frank and loyal and his word is as good as a bond. He is affectionate, devoted and generous, and knows how to win the love of those around him. His mind is essentially materialistic, but does not prevent him from being interested in religion or philosophy in their practical aspects.

Persons born on 3, 12, 21 or 30 of any month or whose sun sign is Sagittarius or Pisces are much influenced by this day.

Women born on Thursday with ascendant Jupiter on Sagittarius or Pisces have almond eyes, light brown hair and expressive blue or hazel eyes. They have flawless complexion charming figures and irresistible confidence.

ARTICLES FOR DONATION : Salt, gram dal, turmeric, gur, yellow cloth.
BEEJ MANTRA : *Om gram grim graum se guravy nameh:*
YOUR DEITY : Shiva, Brahma, Lord Naryana
DIRECTION : North east
LUCKY STONE : Pukhraj to be worn on Thursday morning after Pran Pratishtha.

The shastras mention that any person who recites the above mantra 19,000 times in twenty-one days can fulfill his desires. It will give the native many new and favourable opportunities.

Born on Friday

Persons born on Friday are ruled by Venus. This planet is temperate, moist, fruitful, benefice, magnetic but also negative. Persons born on Friday are kind and benevolent, affectionate and cheerful, and are inclined to pleasure. It is Venus, who in certain circumstances, makes the natives selfish especially those born in the months of January, February, June, July and September.

The card represents women with soft wavy golden hair, plump and lithe figures. It represents the charming goddess of the graces, of games and of laughter, the mother of love, of beauty and of pleasure, the goddess of love. The day represents kindness combined with justice. It is favourable for the imagination and for artistic tasks imparting intellectuality to all things it approaches.

Persons born on 6, 15 or 24 of any month or whose sun signs are Taurus or Libra are much influenced by this day. They are held by the firm hand of justice, sincerity and truth.

Women born on Friday with ascendant Venus on Taurus or Libra are real sweethearts. The position gives a slim form, a rounded and comely face, a well balanced gait, small nose, compelling eyes and silky eye lashes.

ARTICLES FOR DONATION : Ghee, camphor, curd, rice, sugar, white cloth
BEEJ MANTRA : *Aum dhraam dhreem dhraum se shukraye nameh*
YOUR DEITY : Lakshmi
DIRECTION : Southeast
LUCKY STONE : Diamond or firoza to be worn on Friday morning after Pran Pratishtha on the ring finger.

The shastras say that any person who recites the above mantra 6,000 times in seven days can fulfill his desires. It provides the native the kindling spark which helps to solves the most intricate problems of life. The mantra creates a thread which can be followed along the path that leads to success and to the relations one desires. It brings fortune and success through help. Comfort, good fortune and wine are the words of Friday.

Born on Saturday

Persons born on Saturday are ruled by Saturn. This planet is cold, dry and barren. Persons born on Saturday are suspicious, sceptical, lacking in self confidence, but very proud, cautious, studious, patient and industrious. They are dignified, and this quality helps them attain eminent positions after much struggle and difficulty.

The card represents the grandfather, old age, solitude and ancestors. It is a card of good counsel and of prudence which procures moral support, rather than pecuniary help in times of difficulty. It represents intellect, economy, real estate and safe investments, which are the foundation and security of family life. The mind is essentially materialistic, but this does not prevent one from being interested in religion or philosophy in their practical aspects.

Persons born on 8, 17 or 26 of any month or whose sun signs are Capricorn or Aquarius are much influenced by this day. Persons born on Saturday usually live a long life, marked with high ambition and criticism.

Women born on Saturday with ascendant Saturn are usually tall with fine statures; well formed bodies; ruddy complexions, brown eyes an attractive oval shaped faces. The hair is blonde.

ARTICLES FOR DONATION	:	Iron, black nails, mah saboot
BEEJ MANTRA	:	*Om praam preem proum se shanaye nameh*
YOUR DEITY	:	Brahma, Siva
DIRECTION	:	West
LUCKY STONE	:	Blue sapphire to be worn on Saturday morning after Pran Pratishtha.

The shastras say that any person who recites the above mantra 2,300 times in eight days, has good chances of success in politics or some prominent position. The mantra creates a thread between body and soul which gives positive energy. Its recitation helps the native find possibilities of succeeding through his own industry, knowledge and skill. Power, fortune, speculation and occultism are the words of Saturday.

Numbers and Months

Born in January

Persons born in January have a great sense of purpose and ambition to achieve something really lasting and worthwhile in life. They have two vital characteristics which are essential for success—self control and strength of will. And whatever they undertake, they will do it to the best of their ability.

Perseverance is a keyword of their nature, with the result that once they decide to reach a goal, they will persist, until they reach it. It may take some time for them to decide just what they want to do in life, but once they reach a decision, steadfast determination will help them achieve almost anything they set their minds to.

They place importance on other peoples' opinions and they value their trust, confidence and respect. Yet, strangely, they do not take many people into their confidence. Where others are concerned, they sometimes slip into the habit of being suspicious of their motives and so do not make any friends, and prefer one or two trusted and loyal ones, to whom they always will be faithful.

Being influenced by Saturn, they are neither flippant nor superficial, but rather serious, patient, thrifty and stable. These are excellent qualities but they should be careful not to allow an over-cautious attitude cramp initiative, and so prevent them from taking a chance to expand.

Their rather reserved manner will sometimes be misconstrued as aloofness or snobbishness. The reason for this is that they have a keen sense of dignity and formality, and make distinctions between people according to their rank and position in life. Unless they guard against it, they can be quite harsh towards people whom they regard as far beneath them. Not only are they impressed by people who have achieved recognition, they will sometimes deliberately say or do something to impress another person to gain respect.

Their outlook is practical and down to earth and there is likely to be lack of imagination and fun in their nature. They should cultivate their sense of humour and not allow Saturn's over serious and pessimistic outlook to overrule the joy of living. They must learn to be more tolerant of other people whose ideas are not in tune with their own. A little more sympathy and understanding may be needed and this will help to soften and broaden Saturn's tendency to be narrow minded.

January rules the skeletal system, the skin and the knees, so they could be subject to rheumatic pains, broken bones, skin problems or weakness in one or even both the knee joints.

Dark colours appeal to them, particularly dark blue and a navy or bluish shade of violet.

Born in February

Persons born in February are the most humane of all the twelve months and are genial, capable of complete sincerity of purpose and dedication to any particular person or cause. They are not extremists, but their understanding is so broad so as to give the necessary patience and kindness to tolerate other people's follies and idiosyncrasies.

They have a straightforward temperament and disposition which is liked by most people. Easy and genuine friendliness comes naturally to them and their friendships are often long and many in number. Yet, strangely, no matter how well or how long a person has been associated with them, he or she never comes to know them completely. This stems from the complex and unfathomed depths which are latent in the grand sign of Aquarius. Of course, the average person does not realise this and interprets it as a pleasant aloofness in their nature. They give the impression of being slightly detached, without appearing unfriendly or unsympathetic.

They have a strong will and definite opinions; they are not easily swayed by others and will keep to their own ideas with an unshakable determination.

The Saturnine factor is another point that keeps things under control, so there is normally a self contained and tranquil serenity about them which helps them cope with problems, tensions and adverse circumstances. It also causes them to dislike having to rush around. They never make snap decisions unless they are unavoidable. They dislike shoddiness, and no matter what interests them, they are always prepared to spend sufficient time to gain a thorough comprehension of it. They have an inventive and scientific way of looking at things, and unless other factors in the horoscope nullify it, they have the ability to reason clearly and logically. Some of their ideas may be considered too radical, yet they should not allow others to prevent them from capitalising on the opportunities which it presents.

Since they are altruistic, there often seems to be a contradiction, because they are at once naturally friendly, and at the same time loners. There are times when they feel they are a misfit because in some ways, they are ahead of their times.

They could suffer from sprained or weak ankles. Shades of violet, purpule, mauve, lilac and lavender are most likely to be their favourite colours.

Born in March

The influence of Jupiter in this month causes a degree of self confusion. The dualistic nature of the sign pulls them in opposite directions with the result that they can be very undecided about what to do and what they really want. This confusion sometimes makes them feel things are all wrong, but when they try to pinpoint exactly what is wrong, it is difficult, since the confusion is psychological.

They are extremely sensitive and impressionable. The only trouble is that they readily pick up and absorb other people's influence, so it is important for them to associate with the right kind of people, otherwise they could slip into the habit of doing as others do and thinking as others think.

The Jupiterian influences makes them very emotional and feelings play a dominate role in their reactions, both to people and to situations. It also gives them an intuitive, even psychic, nature so they either like or dislike a person without having to reason out their good and bad points. Logical analysis and reasoning do not play a large part in their judgment—rather, they sense things.

They are extremely sympathetic and unlikely to do anything to harm others. However, they should realise that it is sometimes necessary to be cruel in order to be kind.

One of the keynote characteristics of persons born in this month is completeness, which is another way of expressing perfection, and whenever they see a person in trouble or lacking in happiness, health and so on, their desire to assist comes strongly to the fore. They sense their lack of completeness, their lack of perfection, and it is their nature to supply these qualities. Their intentions are good but they are likely to be at a loss when it comes to the best way of giving practical assistance.

They have restless, changeable dispositions, a longing for perfection; in short, they are creatures of varied moods. They dislike having to make important decisions and generally ask other people what to do.

While other people are out playing sports or involved in other busy activities, they prefer peace, quiet and leisure. Unless they guard against this tendency, it can develop into laziness and indifference. Water is likely to hold a special fascination for them, although other factors in the horoscope can easily modify or cancel out this affinity.

Any work or interest which allows plenty of freedom to use their imagination will be in harmony with their natural dispositions. Because March rules the feet, they have problems associated with them, such as corns, bunions, fallen arches and sore, cold, aching or swollen feet.

Shadowy, translucent and deep, mysterious colours appeal to them.

Born in April

Some of the keywords of April are energy, activity, audacity and enterprise, so their nature will be fiery and impulsive with a constant desire to be busy and on the move. They have abundant self confidence in their ability to succeed and no obstacles are too big to tackle, for they have a courageous spirit and will not allow anything to daunt them.

They are frank, forthright and outspoken, sometimes to the point of being rather blunt. They are the type who can quickly become enthusiastic over a new idea but unless other factors in the horoscope lend persistence, they soon find that they have lost this initial enthusiasm and the idea no longer holds appeal. Consequently, there is likely to be a lot of unfinished business in their life—things which had begun on impulse, but which are still waiting to be completed. They should try to cultivate the habit of tying up loose ends and finishing one thing before they begin something else.

The ruling planet Mars makes them bold and impulsive with plenty of on-the-surface self confidence, so that wherever they go, they create an impression. However, some withdrawn and subjective people may find them overwhelming.

'A storm in a tea cup' is a phrase which fits with their temperament. Impulsive, quick and impetuous, they are happiest doing things on the spur of the moment. They get bored with plans.

They may have an abundance of physical vitality but their makeup is better suited to quick, short bursts of activity than to prolonged strain. There is often a surplus of tension and heat in the body, and with Aries on the ascendant, they often suffer from headaches, insomnia and fever. If so stricken, the secret of overcoming them is to learn to relax.

Forceful and determined to get their own way, they can become indignant and even hot tempered when opposed, although they soon forget an argument or a grudge.

Since they are fond of having their own way, they enjoy independence and are happy when in command. They may not be suited for occupations where they have to subjugate their own desires.

There is definite ability to take command in executive positions, but it is essential that they have a back up to maintain a check on their reins, complete what they have left unfinished and also to rectify some of their more impulsive actions.

Mars, their ruling planet, signifies vitality and strength and so, from a health point of view, they do have excellent recuperative powers. However, they should try to avoid burning themselves out with too much activity.

Born in May

the most noticeable characteristics of persons born in May is that they dislike too many changes. A stable and sometimes inflexible mind complements a settled and predictable existence. So, any sudden and unpredicted changes really upset their love of peace and harmony.

They have a loving nature and are almost certainly fond of beauty, music, colour and artistic surroundings. They like pleasure, luxury and have a definite fondness for good food.

Like the bull, they do not get angry easily, when finally stirred, they are capable of violent outbursts. They are stubborn in the face of all opposition, resisting any compromise.

They are thorough in their work because they are practical and pragmatic. For this reason, they may judge things from a purely materialistic point of view. Being very down to earth, they prefer facts and reality to idealism and flights of fancy. However, if by chance their work brings them in touch with fantasy, they will use it—not because they believe in it, but because of the financial returns and business success it brings.

They are possessive of things and people they love. They derive much pressure from collecting and owning beautiful things. However should they feel they are losing their possessive grip, they may experience jealousy and unhappiness.

The ruling planet Venus makes for a quite inflexible nature. Consequently, they have a steadfast determination to plod on and persevere without making too much fuss. Add to this the fact that they are consistent and methodical, and it is easy to see that this zodiacal influence is one indication of worldly success in life. Troubles and difficulties in life may result from unreasonable resistance and stubborn inflexibility, both in matters of human relationships and in business. After all, strong prejudices are fixed thoughts and opinions which control them and their lifestyle. To counter this, they must guard against allowing themselves to think and live in a groove; it is easy for persons born in May to get into a rut.

This month is related to the neck and throat, so they could have some problem in those parts of the body, particularly in early life.

Born in June

One of the most noticeable characteristics of those born in June is the quick manner of walking and constant movements of the hands while talking. They may also include the irritating habit of constant chatter.

They have versatile minds which they use to learn a little about a lot of things, so there is the danger of becoming a jack of all trades, but master of none, unless they make deliberate efforts to stick at something long enough to master it.

Persons born in June have brilliant, ingenious minds. But ingenuity, when combined with restlessness, can also cause inconsistence and lack continuity of purpose. They should guard against letting themselves be satisfied with superficial knowledge about things by learning to concentrate on a single thing at a time.

The nervous system is usually highly strung, and they feel a constant need to be busy, running here and there, phoning someone, jotting down items on notepads and so on. In fact, their minds are always far ahead of their bodies. They must learn to be calm, to give their minds and their nervous systems a chance to unwind. They should learn to sit still, perfectly relaxed, until they reach the point where they do not feel any need to chat or move their hands about restlessly.

They have the twin or double influence of June, so far as they are kind, humane and sympathetic in an intellectual way. But emotionally, they lack depth of feelings when compared with the scale of emotional response possible for some of the other zodiacal signs. Perhaps this is a reason why a fair percentage of people born in June have problems in marriage or marry more than once.

Mercury, the ruling planet of June usually gives fluency in speech and writing and, since it is an intellectual sign, they probably not only enjoy, but are quite proficient at writing, literature or science. June is closely linked with communication, both mental and physical, so their subconscious urge is to make contact with others. Curiosity is one of the keywords and they enjoy investigating new ideas.

Persons born in June on the ascendant can indicate a variety of respiratory problems such as bronchitis, pneumonia or weak lungs. These health problems are particularly noticeable in the early part of life.

Born in July

A noticeable feature of July is sensitivity. Emotional reactions to other people can make people born in July brood over even a small insult or remark, until they imagine it to have gigantic proportions.

Moon, their ruling planet having such sensitive, impressionable qualities, is likely to make them timid and retiring and this cramps their initiatives in making radical changes. They prefer the tested and conservative line of thought and action, so when they are confronted with the need to introduce unusual or unconventional innovations into their lives, they tend to procrastinate them.

This influence of the month, when taken alone and analysed, does not constitute a very robust constitution and often points to faulty action of the digestive system or the stomach, especially in early childhood. Of course, this influence will be modified or accentuated by the position of the sun, moon and planets and the star patterns they form between themselves.

The moon, like the ocean tides which it governs, is changeable and fluctuating. These qualities will manifest in their lives as moods which are bad one day and good bad the next. They must be careful that this moodiness does not develop extremist tendencies and should try to maintain an even balance and remember that moderation in all that they do, is best.

They are good at adapting to changing conditions because they have the knack of being able to sense things beforehand, andthey know how to respond accordingly. They are sympathetic towards people in distress.

They are sentimental, especially where family ties and links with home and partners are concerned. They are the types who always remember birthdays and anniversaries. Close friends are very important and they enjoy nothing more than an evening at home in good company.

Although they may be timid and shy of taking the initiative, especially in physical matters, they can be extraordinarily strong in their mental and moral attitudes and convictions.

Born in August

Their magnetic qualities enable persons born in August to command both the respect and attention of others.

The month is ruled by the Sun and, just as it has control over all the planets and satellites in the solar system, so persons born in August have inherited definite desires and ability to lead, control and organise. They have some of the power and masterful qualities of the Sun, such as self confidence and self possession, and these factors may steer them towards success.

They are self-reliant and self-possessed which makes them thrive on appreciation, approbation and flattery. They are always at their best, give their best and feel a sense of fulfilment when their receive recognition and appreciation. The less favourable aspects of they personality can range from simple ostenting, overdressing and boasting, to pomposity, arrogance and conceit.

They succeed best in positions of authority where they can exercise their organising and administrative abilities. They prefer to lead rather than follow and in their social sphere, they are popular. However, because of these very abilities and their inborn magnetic power, it is all too easy for them to slip into the habit of dominating other people, especially meeker ones who look up to them for assistance.

They are both warm-hearted and generous, particularly towards the people they love, and will give abundantly to people who need their support. In some cases, Leo on the ascendant can cause an excess of these qualities and as a result, they become generous to a fault.

They normally have plenty of faith and hope and are not the types who give in easily to fits of depression and despondency. They are fond of pleasure and luxury and, no matter how limited their resources may be, they have a flair for making something ordinary appear different. This is because they know the value of presentation. Their sense of the dramatic helps them make the most of things by accentuating the right points.

Born in September

Persons born in September have keen powers of discrimination and these, combined with their cool, clear intellectual abilities, gives them accurate insight into most problems and situations. They are born critics so are choosy when it comes to associates. They can stand apart and objectively sum up a person or situation in a detached way; normally they do not allow themselves to be carried away by emotions, so their analysis of any situation is clear and unbiased. Their decisions and opinions will be based on reality.

They enjoy gaining knowledge and can do so without difficulty. When a job has to be done, their careful analysis of it usually leads them to quick solutions to any problem. A combination of tact and diplomacy helps them achieve success. In business affairs, they always watch every detail.

Persons born in this month usually indicate great interest in health matters, but when they are not feeling well, they should try to avoid imagining the worse for themselves. This inborn interest in health complements their hygienic habits. They keep themselves, their clothes, homes and surroundings scrupulously clean.

They are modest and conservative and do not particularly like the limelight, especially when it brings them into close contact with other people. This somewhat virgin-like quality makes them almost indifferent to physical passion and violent emotions and probably accounts for the fact that quite a high percentage of people, who are born with Virgo on the ascendant, prefer to remain single.

Another characteristic is their intense love for details. In everything they do, each separate detail will receive proper attention. This position also favours work which involves small component parts such as watch-making, jewellery, needlework, instrument-making, electric circuits, microscope analysis and so on.

They have sensible and healthy scepticism—it is not bigoted or unreasonable, but more along the lines of discrimination between what is practicable, workable and reasonable, and what is nonsense. If they allow the negative side of their personality to develop, their critical and discriminative faculties will degenerate into constant displays of nagging and fault finding. Their emphasis on details must also be kept well under control because it easily can develop into over- fastidiousness.

Colours such as pale green, lime, olive and some mixtures of yellow and green appeal to them.

Born in October

The most noticeable features about persons born in October is their liking for things in proportion. This rule applies to everything, so that they prefer paintings which are introspective and well-balanced, music which is harmonious rather than discordant, architecture which is symmetrical, clothes which balance and complement their look and personality and so on. Their environment influences them greatly and they will not be happy unless it is harmonious.

Even in their thinking and planning, they like to take time to balance things out, weighing one thing against another and taking a good look at both sides of the situation. For this reason, they appear to be indecisive to those who make snap decisions and they may lose patience with them, especially if they procrastinate things.

Just as the balance can tip easily from one side of the scale to the other, so they can be changeable in both their ideas and their moods. They may give all of their attention to a particular hobby or line of thought and then almost without warning they can drop it, forget all about it as though it never existed and take up a new hobby or entirely different point of view.

They can be very tactful when the occasion demands it and certainly, diplomacy and strategy are strong points associated with them. This stems from their inborn ability to see both sides of the question. With this knowledge, they can cleverly steer their course and manipulate their plans and, when combined with their charm, this enables them to achieve their goals before people even realise how they have done so.

They have a strong sense of justice and will never allow a wrong to go uncorrected. This can sometimes result in other people thinking of them as callous whereas, in reality, they are just being fair. If they extend courtesy to a friend or do a good deed for someone, they expect the person concerned to return the favour.

The ruling planet Venus makes them naturally artistic, with a good eye for design, so their homes will always be tactfully decorated. Beauty and elegance are important to them and they will spare no expense when buying anything which accentuates these qualities.

They are affectionate and make friends easily, so their social life is not only likely to be interesting, but also profitable, providing opportunities for furthering their success. As they have an intense dislike of conflict, tension and discord, most people find it easy to get along with them.

Having well-balanced minds, gives them that rare quality of being able to judge something impartially, because their minds and emotions function as a unit, instead of opposites.

Born in November

Persons born in November have an intensely emotional nature and are capable of deep feelings. As long as their love life runs smoothly, all is well. But if their loved ones should ever deceive them, not only are they never likely to forget it—it is also most unlikely they will ever forgive. At such times, they are their worst enemies as they can suffer agonies of jealousy, resentment and hatred.

The influence of Mars gives them a concentered and intense nature in which tenacity is a fundamental quality. They have plenty of determination and unflinching courage to achieve their goals. Their thoroughness, drive and fixed purpose will take them far along the road to success, but there is perhaps one drawback to being so intense—they tend to look upon life as a battle to be won. They should just be careful that their self-discipline does not replace light-hearted fun.

No problem is too formidable for them to tackle; a challenge or an obstacle creates an outlet for their dynamic constructive or destructive abilities. They know what they want and will not allow anyone or anything to stand in their way.

They have strong likes and dislikes and cannot be persuaded easily to change plans or opinions. They have inflexible will power with great self-reliance and this may be one of the reasons why they tend not to trust or rely on other people.

They are willing to work hard and long to achieve their goals and, being secretive, they do not normally divulge all their plans. They may reveal some of the facts, but they always keep their trump cards hidden.

They demand the utmost from themselves and when in a position of authority, they expect the same from others. So they are likely to come up against harsh criticism unless they learn to relax the reins of discipline and become more tolerant.

Any trouble they may experience in life is likely to be the result of too much emotional intensity or jealousy, for they are capable of experiencing the extremes of love and hate and their emotions can tear them to pieces. Unless nipped in the bud, this can lead to them treating other people harshly, especially those who serve them or who are subordinates.

They are closely allied to the principle of death and destruction, and it is remarkable how many times I have seen children born in this month take a delight in dealing sadistically with insects, animals and even their own possessions. This influence occasionally can turn in on itself, just as the scorpion can sting itself to death. And the result is a person who subconsciously destroys his or her own success or happiness.

As far as the physical body is concerned, November is related to sexual organs and reproduction which can indicate an over emphasis on sex or even some type of physical problem involving the reproductive organs.

Born in December

A strong desire for expansion is one of the hallmarks of the nature of persons born in December. The avenues through which they will seek this expansion will depend on date of birth but it will be on one or more of these three levels: their physical environment and surroundings; their mental interests, knowledge and learning; spiritual unfolding and expansion of the consciousness. Another strongly marked characteristic which naturally accompanies their driving urge to expand is a strong sense of independence and a great love of freedom. They will not tolerate anyone or anything restricting their freedom or placing limitations on their thoughts or activities.

As far as close relationships are concerned, the influence of this month can cause problems, unless they are recognised early and handled carefully. The reason is that when marriage or any other close partnership is entered into, it automatically imposes a tie and a certain amount of restriction on their freedom and independence. After the initial romance fades and marriage becomes a practical affair, they come to resent the fact that they are no longer independent. Unless they take full control of their impulsive nature, it can lead to problems in married life.

Of course, it also can cause the other extreme, where the person refuses to give up his or her freedom and does not marry at all. Naturally where the success of failure or marriage is concerned, the influence of the birth number must be considered. Certainly not every person born in this month destined to a broken marriage but, nevertheless, it is an influence which needs careful handling.

They have a keen intelligence and a rather colourful, enthusiastic personality, but they must check the tendency to be over-optimistic and over-confident, especially in business and financial affairs where practical thinking is essential. They are open and candid and, although sometimes abrupt in their manners as a result of their impulsive qualities, they generally like people to act in a 'proper' manner, since they themselves usually behave according to the rules of etiquette. Though the positive influence of Jupiter makes them generous, just and honest, they can tolerate people who are underhanded or deceptive.

Sciatica, rheumatic pains, liver trouble and varicose veins are some of the possible ailments associated with them. This month also rules the hips and thighs, so these areas could be affected by falls, cuts and bruises.

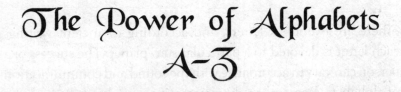

The Power of Alphabets A-Z

There are twenty-six letters, and according to ancient writings each letter is devoted to a particular star/planet. The success of a person can vary in accordance with the sound and communication of alphabets. Remember, the success of a man depends upon the number of letters and its compatibility with his date of birth. As one's attire, style and hair style etc change one's look, similarly, one's name and its spelling play an important role in changing one's destiny.

A
(AMBITION)

People whose names begin with 'A' reckon their own capability to conquer the forces of heaven. They are non-conformists as far as their goals and personal ambitions are concerned. These are most definitive in their minds. It represents *aum*.

B
(BLISS)

They are the kind of the people who are capable of holding on to secrets. They are diplomatic and will be able to win their way through effective arguments. Their quick wit, perceptiveness and intelligence will win them a wide group of friends. They can attain excellence in the field of academics.

C
(CELEBRATION)

Its outline denotes an arc which symbolises a powerful and creative temperament. People whose names begin with 'C' have the motivation and drive to achieve their aims and move up the social ladder with speed. They may not always be an academic sort, but have the ability to learn and apply their knowledge suitably. They should respect the feelings and emotions of their friends and relatives; it would give them greater security and something to value later in life.

D
(DEDICATION)

They are closely and intricately linked with their jobs and personal life. They mostly keep to themselves, are idealists and often get lost in their thoughts and fantasies. They should remember that in order to attain anything in life, they should act rather than just think. Their persistence and determination enables them to attain all that they want.

E
(ENTHUSIASM)

E has three bars and hence symbolises activity on the basis of merit and significant development on both mental and spiritual levels. People whose names begin with 'E' have a lot of enthusiasm and strength. They are gifted with an 'I can' temperament. This approach is their guiding force in everything. If they make up their mind, there is nothing that can stand in their way or stop them. It symbolises *shakti swaropan*.

ℱ
(Flexibility)

The five 'barred' letters show that they have a strong urge to be loved and cared for. They are somewhat temperamental and anxious. They are gifted with a flair for language and have no trouble in expressing themselves clearly and precisely.

G
(Glory)

Motivation and ambition are their strongest traits and are responsible for leading them to prosperity. Nothing stands in their way and everything is easy for them to achieve. Filled with a lot of energy, eagerness and zest, they use all their reserves to achieve their goals. They are always willing to help.

ℋ
(Harmony)

This bar represents poise and balance. Driven by aspirations, and the desire to rise higher, they have a tendency to please others. They could be hurt or disillusioned. They simply move ahead and give their best to achieve that goal. They have a career that would excite them and the enable them to express their aesthetic and imaginative sides. In mantras, *ha* means Shiva.

ℐ
(Industrious)

'I' symbolises a temperament that is observant, attentive and enthusiastic. They have immense energy and motivation. They concentrate on achieving their own personal and professional goals. Trust me, their efforts indeed bear sweet fruits. Pythagoras identified this alphabet with God's head. The alphabet 'I' is indivisible. This alphabet represents optimism, hope and belief in oneself.

J
(JUBILATION)

Crowds and chaos tend to irk them and they have the tendency of becoming moody and dismal right in the midst of a party. They have a mind that is easily influenced and therefore when it comes to relationships, they often invest their time and energy in people who are undeserving and then, end up feeling sorry for themselves.

K
(KARAMYOGI)

The alphabet 'K' represents a dignified and independent profile. Good orators, they have the advantage of using words to win their way. They have high hopes for themselves and work hard to ensure that those hopes are realised. For them, success is important, since it helps them to earn respect. They enjoy the appreciation that others shower on them. In the mantras, *ka* means Krishna, Kamdev and Kali.

L
(LEADER)

Although they are not very generous, people whose names begin with 'L' are not terribly selfish either. They extremely focused on achieving their goals and are strong fighters. Their business and financial acumen is strong and they also have a dominant aesthetic streak.

M
(MAJESTIC)

'M' indicates a life filled with radical changes. Tranquility is something that is a rare phenomenon in their lives. Sweeping changes and constant turmoil are associated with these people. They have a constitution that prepares them for all the unexpected occurrences that may take place. They enjoy being appreciated and acknowledged. However, for them, the real rewards of life is love and warmth rather than material goods.

N
(NOBLE)

They thrive on being acknowledged and rewarded. They are practical and understand the importance of success and prosperity. People are often found to be happy with marriages of convenience rather than of love. They may not show their feelings most of the time, yet love their partners deeply.

O
(OPTIMISTIC)

The alphabet, 'O', endows the individual with curiosity for news. They have blunt, straightforward tongues, and as a result, may end up hurting a few friends and colleagues. They should try to be more considerate and should always, remember that what goes up, always comes down.

P
(Passionate)

People whose names begin with 'P' rise, succeed and prosper solely on the basis of their merit. It is only when they apply their minds, intelligence and thirst for knowledge, that they are able to succeed. Based on the strength of their intellect, analysis and reason, they are able to make a mark for themselves in the fields of medicine, science, astrology, law and similar fields.

Q
(Quality)

They should learn to control nitpicking, otherwise they will get extremely lonely and dissatisfied. Although they hold a very gracious and efficient impression of themselves, the truth is that they are extremely emotional and are always on an emotional rollercoaster.

R
(Righteousness)

'R' indicates a strong streak of self-determination in everything that they do. They have great regard for truth and integrity. They are righteous and command respect wherever they go. As such, they are able to rise high and succeed. They should just remember that they need to mingle their beliefs with reality in a sensible manner.

S
(SOVEREIGNTY)

'S' indicates an influential and dominating character. They have determination and persistence. These overshadow their flair for eloquence. Although they are intelligent and influenced by feelings, yet this is not apparent to those who know them only from a distance. They are profound individuals and may not even be aware about their own strengths and weaknesses.

T
(TRADITIONAL)

They are quite rigid and stubborn with their habits and routines. They are able to justify their reactions and temperament, yet there is no doubt about the fact that they are strongly obstinate. The good thing is that they are able to convince others about the logic behind their thoughts and opinions.

U
(UNIVERSAL)

Liberal and broadminded, they welcome new information and soak it up eagerly. They are able to deal with the many problems of life in an efficient and pleasant manner. They also have creative imagination and it is important that they develop it constantly. Being good diplomats, they maintain a cordial relationship with people who matter without going overboard.

V
(Vivacious)

They have certain characteristics that make them interesting persons to interact with. They are moody and temperamental. They never give the impression of being selfish. 'V' indicates receptiveness, and stands for victory.

W
(Worship)

'W' indicates that the individual has a flair for theatre and drama. This talent combined with a keen intellect and an inherent charisma results in a winning package. Their perseverance and determination ensure that they resolve all their problems with grace and ease.

X
(X-mas)

'X' indicates a strong streak of obstinacy. This obstinacy, as they grow, changes into strong willpower and rationality. They find that they have a magnetism, which people respect and are drawn towards. They are ready to take on any task and complete it in a responsible manner.

Y
(Yoga)

People whose names begin with 'Y' have keen interest in observing people around them. They are charming, fascinating and enjoy a high-profile, well-paying job. They rely on their popularity and charisma with the larger section of society. Hence, they do well in the field of marketing.

3
(ZENITH)

They are ethical and hardworking and they also have the tendency to be obstinate. They do not let anything stand in their path to success and overcome most obstacles easily, and with integrity.

Intense and devoted, they treat their personal relationships with seriousness and a slightly demanding nature. They are successful socially, personally and professionally.

Psychoanalysis of Names

I have been doing research work on numbers and its influence over our lives. Every alphabet has its own occult power. A slight rotation of any telephone number can create lot of confusion Similarly any alphabet added or subtracted to one's name can create miracles in terms of one's career, business and love life etc. Numerology also helps in holistic healing of people.

Ancient seers and numerologists have assigned certain powers or occult powers to each alphabet. According to Helign Hitchcole and Kabla, the numerical value of each alphabet is as under:

A	B	C	D	E	F	G	H	I
J	K	L	M	N	O	P	Q	R
S	T	U	V	W	X	Y	Z	
1	2	3	4	5	6	7	8	9

My own research work and personal experience reveals that the system followed by Cherio and Montrose is much better and gives a dramatic effect in this modern era. They have applied the following values for each alphabet:

1	2	3	4	5	6	7	8
A	B	C	D	E	U	O	F
I	K	G	M	H	V	Z	P
Q	R	L	T	N	W		
J	S	X					

A well-known film director, Yash Chopra, has given us an insight into the recurrence of number games in his professional life.

He christened the name of his film:

KABHI   KABHIE
2 1 2 5 1   2 1 2 5 1 5   = 27

By adding the extra 'E' in the second instance, the numerical value comes to 27.

People who are number 27 natives are influenced by the Moon and Neptune and hence, have a strong sense of fairness and are honest and straightforward in everything they do. They do well in fields of administration, government offices and politics. Benevolent and compassionate, they share their time and money willingly. They are also determined and dynamic and experience great fortune in their latter years.

In the case of absence of 'E', the numerical value comes to:

KABHI   KABHI
2 1 2 5 1   2 1 2 5 1   = 22

which will read as:

Number 22 natives are influenced by the Moon solely and therefore, are independent in action and spirit and often, are different from the rest, they hold radical views and need to work hard at adjusting with others. When aspected positively, number 22 endows the natives with fame and fortune. But when negatively aspected, they are affected by scandals and scams. It is important that they pay attention to their own instincts or intuition.

Now let us consider the case of NAPOLEON BUONAPARTE who later changed his name to NEPOLEON BONAPARTE

NAPOLEON BUONAPARTE
51873575 2675181245   = 82

The meaning of 82 is as follows:

The influence of the Moon along with Saturn endows number 82 natives with confidence, independence and innovativeness. They are successful and prosperous. However, they need to make the required effort. This number makes capable lawyers, doctors, teachers and architects. They should avoid indulging in gambling and reckless speculation.

NEPOLEON BONAPARTE
51873575 275181245   = 76

The meaning of 76 is as follows:

Idealistic and dreamy, the natives spend a fair amount of time in daydreaming and thinking about the future rather than taking concrete action. Though they may not have a lot of determination, there would be a fair amount of self-control which enables them to achieve most goals and ambitions. This is a number that denotes influence and authority and hence, is quite fortunate for the future.

Accordingly, each number from 1 to 108 has its specific influence are one's character in terms of money; health, marriage and career. However, this must coincide with one's date of birth. Likewise, the number of the house one lives in, should be a number which has affinity with one's birth date. A number 8 man should not live in a number 4 house or a number in series of 4, 13, 22, 31, 40, 49 and so on. One can also apply the science of numbers to towns, cities, cars, lottery, etc. If used correctly, it can aid one in maligning or even offsetting the unfavourable possibilities and of assisting those constructive and helpful in nature. I understand, my esteem readers can definitely derive the full benefit from numerology. The significance the numbers 1 to 108 is given.

Calculation of Your
Destiny Number

Suppose one's name is Seema Singh and date of birth is 31. 10. 1976

Step 1: Date of Birth

31. 10. 1976

When added up, it comes to 28

The natives of number 28 are under the Moon-Saturn association, which is also referred to as the 'Cycle of Saturn'. This phenomenon would result in certain limitations. However, individuals are able to grow and progress in life. They should guard against possessiveness, both at home and at work, and should not place their trust easily in untrustworthy friends. Money is not very stable but there is no acute shortage of resources. Hard work and devotion to their goals ensures that the native has a good life.

Step 2: Psychoanalysis of the name

S E E M A   S I N G H
3 5 5 4 1   3 1 5 3 5   = 35

The number 35 reads:

Number 35 is a number which endows natives with an intense and profound temperament. As a result of which, they want to spend time on their own and introspect and reflect on the mysteries of life. They are also academically inclined and rise high in society and in their profession. The natives enjoy travelling and are fortunate in most aspects.

Seema Singh was born on 31-10-1976. As such, number 35 is not compatible with her destiny number. She is a Scorpio and she is governed by number 9. So when 'A' added is added to her name the total comes to 36 and results in strong vibration of the name and the sun sign.

SEEMAA   SINGH
3 5 5 4 1 1   3 1 5 3 5   = 36

The number 36 reads:

This number is fortunate for the individual in more ways than one and though the natives have to put in a lot of hard work, the rewards are assured. Because of their temperament, the natives make good administrators or senior executives and are also able to lead a life of comfort and contentment at home.

My friend Sandeep Diwan was born on 2. 12. 1965

Step 1: Date of Birth 2-12-1965

When added up, it comes to 26

Natives of number 26 are influenced by the Moon and Venus, and are intelligent, energetic and successful in most endeavours. They are also gifted with keen perception and make successful astrologers, healers, scientists, doctors and lawyers. Whether aspected positively or negatively, this number brings prosperity, success and growth to the natives. However, they should guard against confusion, misunderstanding and conflict, especially on the domestic front.

Step 2: Psychoanalysis of a business name:

CHITRALOK
3 5 1 4 2 1 3 7 2 = 28

The number 28 reads:

The natives of number 28 are under the Moon-Saturn association, which is also referred to as the 'Cycle of Saturn'. This phenomenon results in certain limitations, however, individuals would be able to grow and progress in life. They should guard against possessiveness both at home and at work, and should not place their trust easily in untrustworthy people. Money is not very stable; however, there is no acute shortage of resources. Hard work and devotion towards their goals would ensure that the natives have a good life.

Sandeep Diwan was born on 02-12-1965 as such number 28 is not compatible with his destiny number. He is a Sagittarian and as such he is governed by number, When 'R' is added to his business name, the total comes to 30; which leads to a strong vibration of the name and the sun sign.

CHITRRALOK
3 5 1 4 2 2 1 3 7 2   = 30

This particular number is under the vibrations of Jupiter and Pluto and because of that, endows the natives with a life of hard work and effort. They have to overcome obstacles in order to achieve goals, especially in the early part of their lives. There is a fair amount of travelling that they may have to undertake and also get married only when they feel adequately settled. Although the path to success may be tough, the natives will surely enjoy success, fame and fortune.

Octaves of Numbers
1–9

Octave of Number 1

1
(AMBITION)

It represents the leader, the husband, the father, the political ruler, and helps natives acquire the assistance and collaboration of powerful people. When the cards are read, it symbolises the Day, since it gives radiation, prosperity and permanence. Power, authority, influence and control characterise them.

10
(SPECULATION)

The number 10 is an uncertain number. The combination of Sun and Pluto tends to determine the natives' fortune, based on their own plans and wishes. As a result, there may be frequent ups and downs in the natives' lives. However, at the same time, the natives are endowed with several admirable qualities such as self-esteem, energy and the ability to be a role model for others. The natives are advised to exercise caution in decision-making.

19
(AUTHORITY)

Brimming with vitality, magnetism and kindness, natives of

number 19 are influenced by the Sun and Mars. They have intelligent and, intuitive minds and are able to grasp things quickly. Optimistic, cheerful and confident, they have the ability to forge ahead and even if they lose their cool at times, they bounce back quickly. They tend to do well in fields of medicine, construction, architecture, business and will climb up the ladder surely and steadily. Their love life would also be happy. However, they must be careful of getting over-possessive. Their hard work brings them a great deal of recognition and rewards.

28
(INFLEXIBILITY)

The natives of number 28 are under the Moon-Saturn association, also referred to as the 'Cycle of Saturn'. This phenomenon results in certain limitations. However, individuals are able to grow and progress in life. They should guard against possessiveness both at home and at work and should not place their trust easily in untrustworthy people. Money is not very stable. However, there is no acute shortage of resources. Hard work and devotion towards their goals ensures that the natives have a good life.

37
(CONFIDENCE)

The influence of the planet Jupiter endows natives with motivation, intelligence and compassion. As a result, the natives are able to achieve their hearts' desires and succeed in nearly everything they undertake. They should guard against the negative influence of Mars and Saturn.

46
(DETERMINATION)

This number makes the natives authoritative and strong-willed, because of which they may get involved in conflicts and confusion with colleagues and friends. In matters of the heart, natives would be quite fortunate. This is a number of influence and power. At the same time, the natives must weigh each decision carefully and then step forward.

55
(RESEARCH)

In number 55, the double Mercury endows natives with popularity and recognition in both personal and professional lives. Careful, smart and compassionate, natives win friends and hearts wherever they go. The natives are also independent and make good and sensible decisions.

64
(VIGOUR)

Number 64 natives may experience some initial hardships in achieving their goals and ambitions, however, after they turn forty-five, things will flow relatively smoothly and will enable them to build a secure and stable future. Most importantly, they will be able to deal with problems and challenges in a positive manner and not get defeated by them. The fate of the natives is largely determined by their attitude and outlook.

73
(INDUSTRIOUS)

The vibrations of Jupiter endow natives with astute minds and they are able to understand their goals and also plan a strategy to achieve them. Natives are determined, creative and work their way up the ladder through slow but steady means. This particular number is also lucky for long-distance travel and the future.

82
(HEADSTRONG)

The influence of the Moon along with Saturn endows number 82 natives with confidence, independence and innovativeness. They are successful and prosperous, however, need to make the required efforts. This number makes capable lawyers, doctors, teachers and architects. They should avoid indulging in gambling and reckless speculation.

91
(HONEST)

Number 91 natives exert a great deal of influence over others and are able to demonstrate great mental and physical endurance in the toughest of conditions. However, natives should guard against being too argumentative or quarrelsome. Natives are loving, kind and are emotional. In matters of love and marriage, they are faithful and passionate.

100
(HONOURS)

In the number 100, the Sun is magnified to the maximum degree, and when combined with double Pluto, bestows the natives with strong willpower, diligence, and sharp minds. The natives are warm, loving and friendly because of which friends are also helpful and considerate. The natives should guard against forming extremely strong preferences.

Octave of Number 2

2
(HONEST)

This is symbolic of fortune, the unknown, travel, heritage and transformation from a spiritual point of view. The natives also cherish a love for travel and journeys. Introverted, perceptive, creative and versatile, the natives have a great deal of patience and bear unpleasant situations for a long time. However, they are very quick to change when they cross the limit of endurance. They also have an immense ability to lie back and simply let the world pass them by.

11
(IMAGINATIVE)

The number 11 is a strong number, especially, due to the combination of Sun and Sun. Independent and distinctive, the natives stand apart in a crowd and have the willpower and fortitude to achieve anything that their hearts' desire. Due to the strength of their personalities, there may be some amount of conflict. In matters of love and romance, the individual may have to make compromises. Accidents would pose a threat to life.

20
(Changeable)

Number 20 natives are influenced by the Moon and the planet Pluto. As a result, they have an affinity with water and travelling. They also enjoy mountains and peaceful environs and get bored with routine and regular work. They are compassionate and imaginative. They are also protective towards those they love and do not take undue risks in business and investments. Although they are patient, their anger is fiery. They should devote themselves to their careers and their families, and happiness will surely come their way.

29
(Devoted)

This particular combination of Moon and Mars endows the natives with creative and intuitive temperaments. Sensitive and sentimental, they need to work on being more practical and realistic, especially in matters of the heart. At times, they may feel that they are being pulled in opposite directions by their own desires and needs. The natives might be inclined towards disorders of the nervous system and may be taken advantage of by undependable friends and partners. They must prepare well for the future.

38
(Friendly)

This particular number endows the natives with strong business acumen and also a knack to make money out of anything. Love and romance is a positive influence in the natives' lives. However, they need to be more adjusting towards friends and well-wishers.

47
(Optimistic)

Freedom-loving and courageous, the natives of number 47 are able to earn fame and fortune by following the path of honesty and sincerity. If aspected negatively, the natives are able to achieve a great deal in life. The influence of Neptune makes the natives capable and diligent, especially in creative pursuits. They succeed primarily by applying intellect, ability and common-sense.

56
(Dependable)

The number allows natives to earn profits, especially, from speculative ventures. Professionally, natives succeed from hard work as much as from good luck. They should guard against disloyal friends and also be careful in matters of the heart.

65
(Highly principled)

The number 65 is influenced by the combination of Venus and Mercury and therefore has a positive impact on the natives' intellect and keenness. The natives are also influenced favourably by people from foreign countries. From the point of view of marriage, the alliance would be quite profitable, financially as well as emotionally. The natives should guard against being reckless and rash.

74
(INTELLIGENT)

Number 74 natives are tender-hearted and peaceful in their outlook. However, they are not quick to forgive and forget. They simply bide their time till they can get even with the person who hurt them. Natives are also interested in mysticism and other fascinating subjects. Professionally, they do well if they work with full sincerity and interest. They must guard against being reckless. The number is lucky for the future.

83
(PATIENT)

Number 83 natives are somewhat aloof and detached. However, they have kind and loving hearts and are willing helpers. This attitude is beneficial in professional endeavours and their tranquility ensures that their plans are best known to themselves only. Wealth, fame and fortune come a little late in life.

92
(COMMANDER)

Number 92 natives are influenced by the vibrations of the Moon and Mars. This is a suitable position for the Moon and makes natives independent and decisive. They are helpful, and depend on themselves to earn a living and make a name. The number also ensures that the natives are authoritative and able to command the attention of those around them.

101
(PROTECTIVE)

The combination of double Sun and Pluto empowers the natives with the instinct to avoid most of life's hurdles and progress at a rapid pace in life. Colleagues, associates and friends also motivate, and assist the natives and hence life is fulfilling and enjoyable.

Octave of Number 3

3
(PRACTICAL)

Influential and dominating, this is a planet that is responsible for creating diplomats; officials of religious bodies, government personnel and which also exercises a lot of power over business people and others who are in the limelight. They have a strong drive to achieve honour and name in the society. This may at times be seen as a tendency towards pride and conceit.

12
(FRIENDLY)

Natives of number 12 is ruled by the combination of the Sun and Moon and is one filled with the desire to succeed and rise high. They make influential friends and equally influential enemies. Fortunate and helpful, these individuals have the ability to guide others and give sound advice. They are also quite intelligent and invest their money with caution and prudence. They should be careful of animals, especially, reptiles.

21
(SACRIFICING)

Influenced by the Moon and the Sun, number 21 natives are optimistic and persistent in everything they do. They succeed in fields related to creative arts, music, literature as well as law. Fame and fortune are theirs if they put in the required amount of hard work and effort. Benevolent and kind-hearted, they often take a stand against wrongdoings and corruption. They are very patient, though not with people who have little or no sense and do not suffer fools gladly. They are dedicated to their goals and aspirations and spend a great deal of time in their realisation. However, they should try and balance their personal and professional lives in order to bring about harmony and happiness.

30
(HUMANITARIAN)

This particular number comes under the vibrations of Jupiter and Pluto, and endows the natives with a life of hard work. They have to overcome obstacles in order to achieve their goals, especially, in the early part of their lives. There is a fair amount of travelling that they may have to undertake and also get married only when they feel adequately settled. Although the path to success may be tough, natives will surely enjoy success, fame and fortune.

39
(ORGANISED)

This number has the protection of Jupiter and bestows the natives with rewards, recognition and a strong character. They are able to reach high goals, depending upon the aspect of the 3rd and 9th Houses. Financially, too, their goals will be met and they will lead a comfortable life.

48
(ENTHUSIASTIC)

This is a number that endows the natives with discretion and ambition. They are able to succeed in fields requiring both tact and talent. Generous and loving, the natives do well in business and also make loyal spouses and genuine friends.

57
(PROSPEROUS)

The influence of Mercury and Neptune bestows number 57 natives with strong relationships and loyal friends who are advisors, guides and motivators. Compassionate and generous, the natives are faithful spouses and thoughtful partners. Hard work and effort will surely lead to success and fortune.

66
(ROMANTIC)

This number is quite a fortunate number for individuals from a creative standpoint. The natives are pleasant and have good aesthetic sense and are most comfortable in an artistic environment. The future is hopeful and success is assured in professional and social spheres.

75
(DEPENDABLE)

This number is profitable from a financial standpoint and brings about a gainful venture or job for the native, which is also safe and secure. However, in matters of love and romance, natives have to overcome some hurdles and obstacles. The natives are also somewhat laid back and do not jump into anything impulsively.

84
(CONSIDERATE)

Influenced to some extent by Jupiter, number 84 is a number of harmony and equilibrium which gives the natives wealth, success and a good social life. However, all aspects are balanced and the natives are overly influenced by any one of them. Generally, natives do not take easily to hard labour and prefer a life of ease and comfort. They are graceful and charming in their manners. This is a lucky number for the future.

93
(BRAVE)

The influence of Mars in number 93 indicates that the natives have a sound business sense and are active and confident. They also have analytical minds and are able to plan and strategise effectively. Although the natives have to work hard initially, things smoothen out eventually. Yet, they must always be careful and control their tempers.

102
(Sensitive)

Number 102 natives have a strong practical approach and are able to achieve professional and personal milestones. However, they need to work on their self-esteem and be more assertive in order to lead a life of dignity and strength. In case the Sun is afflicted by either Venus or Mars, the natives would be indecisive and changeable.

Octave of Number 4

4
(CREATIVE)

It is responsible for bringing about unusual and uncharacteristic behaviour and situations in the life of the natives. It is a definite indicator of self-reliance and rebelliousness. However, it also happens to radiate a certain kind of unique brilliance. Others could well consider natives unconventional.

13
(LOYAL)

Number 13 natives are individuals who have strength of the mind and as well as strength of the body. They are able to work their way up the ladder using intelligence and hard work. Since they have strong preferences, they also tend to get into arguments and misunderstandings with others. Moreover, they work better on their own and hence, should avoid getting into partnerships and the like. As far as money is concerned, they both earn and lose money in ways that are out of the ordinary.

22
(HONOURABLE)

Number 22 natives are influenced by the Moon solely and

therefore, are independent in action and spirit and are often different from the rest. They hold radical views and need to work hard at adjusting with others. When aspected positively, number 22 endows the natives with fame and fortune. But when negatively aspected, they are affected by scandals and scams. It is important that they pay attention to their own instincts or intuition.

31
(CHARMING)

This number denotes a desire to get rich quick and also move from one place to another. The natives are under the vibrations of Jupiter and the Sun and have to tackle hardships and criticism from family members and friends. As a result, their lives may witness many changes. Professional and money matters need extra care and the natives must save money.

40
(SECRETIVE)

The number endows the natives with minds that are analytical, astute and perceptive. Therefore, the natives do well in fields of law, medicine, journalism and similar areas. Innovative and self-reliant, the natives are kind and hard-working, because of which success is not difficult to come by.

49
(VISIONARY)

Natives of number 49 are blessed with marital happiness. However, they have to demonstrate their feelings and sincerity to their partners. They are gentle and loving towards others and may not have to try hard to win the affection of their partners. Professionally, too, they are able to progress and reach their goals in time.

58
(Success)

Number 58 symbolises a gentle and amiable temperament with a profound sense of creativity. Peace-loving, the natives are not the violent sort, and take things as they come. Such individuals make good doctors, lawyers and religious leaders. However, they must work on being more assertive and not become too placid.

67
(Constructive)

Number 67 natives are amicable individuals who are able to make and keep friends with ease and genuineness. In business and professional undertakings as well, they are able to progress and profit through their contacts. They have sound financial acumen and therefore, are able to establish a secure future for themselves.

76
(Receptive)

Idealistic and dreamy, the natives spend a fair amount of time in daydreaming and thinking about the future rather than taking concrete action. Though they may not have a lot of determination, there is a fair amount of self-control which enable them to achieve most goals and ambitions. This is a number that denotes influence and authority and hence, is quite fortunate for the future.

85
(PROUD)

Natives are easily influenced and need to be more assertive in order to be happier with their lives. They should not take small things to heart and be more accepting and adjusting. Since they have an introspective temperament, they may not be very expressive and this may cause some trouble as far as love and marriage are concerned. Natives do not conform to rules blindly, but only if they make some sense. They should refrain from gambling.

94
(POTENT)

Number 94 natives are influenced by Mars and Uranus which enables them to build a financially secure future, based on their own efforts. They are filled with profitable and unconventional ideas and hence are quite broadminded. Their style of working may not be the most orderly, however, there is sense in the chaos surrounding them.

103
(ADVENTUROUS)

Analytical and logical, number 103 natives are able to acquire a great deal of knowledge in next to no time. As a result, they have a flair for business, engineering and even the arts. Brave as well as compassionate, the natives are able to help others and are also helped by them in return.

Octave of Number 5

5
(BRIGHT)

It has a significant effect in the fields of commerce, medicine, language and composing. Since it is realistic; it influences the natives' fortune, wealth, and real estate. It makes them good humoured and quick at repartee. They have investigative and logical minds.

14
(ADAPTABLE)

Natives of number 14 are influenced by a combination of the Sun and Uranus. Therefore, it is not surprising that they are quick on the uptake and are also good leaders with plenty of tact and discretion. Business and professions suit them and they do very well in fields in which they interact with people and have to do some amount of planning and strategising. Being good speakers and writers, fame and fortune come to them without much problem.

23
(INVENTIVE)

Number 23 is influenced by the Moon and Jupiter. The natives have sophisticated and tactful temperaments as well as intelligent minds. Though they may seem timid and unpretentious, they often achieve a great deal of success and fame in their careers as well as in their social circle. This number brings many positive chances for the natives and is beneficial for speculation and money matters.

32
(COMMUNICATIVE)

Number 32 signifies rapidity in everything—thoughts, words, actions and acumen. The natives are able to create their future, according to their actions and ideas. However, they must guard against the meddling of other people. Logical and perceptive, they are sociable and popular with nearly everyone. If aspected negatively, they may get into wrong company and addictive behaviour. This number is lucky for the future.

41
(VIVACIOUS)

The main feature of number 41 is highly developed intelligence and a strong streak of independence. The natives do not want to be bound by rules and regulations. They want to achieve goals by the shortest methods possible. Courage and common sense enable them to keep rivals and opponents at arms' length.

50
(OPEN-MINDED)

The natives of number 50 have a sense of fairness and charismatic temperaments. They gain from monetary dealings and from political ambitions. Natives also have a fondness for children and lead a relatively happy married life.

59
(ANALYTICAL)

This number is fortunate for intellectual and mental matters and endows the individual with a balanced and perceptive mind. They are realistic as well as idealistic and also pay attention to the small details of life. If aspected from Mars, the natives may be somewhat dominating. Since the natives are quite inclined towards spiritualism, financial matters may tend to get somewhat ignored. However, they will have a fair share of fame and fortune.

68
(LEADERSHIP)

Natives of number 68 are influenced by Venus and Saturn, and hence, are quite aggressive in their approach. While they are basically intelligent and practical, they do not want to be opposed by anyone. However, their sense of fairness do not allow them to be prejudiced. Health and marriage need attention. Money matters are profitable for the natives.

77
(IMAGINATIVE)

Number 77 natives benefit from a financial standpoint and also enjoy a place of importance in social and professional circles. Though they may not be the top boss, yet their positions are these of distinction and authority. Natives are charismatic,

powerful and perceptive individuals who are able to carve out
their own destiny.

86
(MAGICAL)

The natives of number 86 wish to lead a life of peace and
tranquility. Happy go lucky and compassionate, they are content
with their marriage and children. A mystic number, natives are
creative and have a flair for the dramatic. When aspected
negatively, chances are that natives might get entangled in bad
company.

95
(RESOURCEFUL)

The combination of Mars with Mercury endows the natives
with quickness of mind and talkative temperaments. They are
able to map out their own plans in life and carry it out
successfully. Relationships are strong, yet the natives should
guard against shallow friends and associates.

104
(ENJOYS CHALLENGES)

Number 104 natives are dreamy, idealistic and if born in a
wealthy family, lead a life of comfort. Otherwise, they need to
become practical and start working hard in order to enjoy the
basic comforts of life. Since the natives are inherently creative
and artistic, they make good poets, artists and writers.

Octave of Number 6

6
(MUSICAL)

This is a planet that signifies beautiful things and emotions of love and passion. Venus symbolises warmth, friendliness, relationships and a fondness for music and poetry. It bestows the individual with several favourable attributes. The natives are generous, loving, tender, happy and enjoy the comforts of life.

15
(ROMANTIC)

Ruled by the Sun and Mercury, number 15 natives are artistic, creative and love to surround themselves with beauty in every aspect, including self and people. Love and romance are an integral part of their lives. Financially too, they are quite fortunate and often come into money from unexpected sources. High on energy and fond of activity, they need to pay special attention to their nerves and take adequate rest.

24
(ARTISTIC)

Number 24 natives symbolise charisma and creativity. They have a keen inclination towards art, music, literature and drama.

They are also able to appeal to the opposite sex and hence are quite popular. Marriage and love bring happiness and prosperity, especially for women. They should be careful of excessive spending and should save some for later years. They are also sociable and enjoy entertaining and making new friends.

33
(STEADFAST)

Number 33 is influenced by double Jupiter and endows the natives with a fondness for games, sports, and simply being outdoors. Living in the open and being one with nature give the natives great joy. They believe in leading a simple, natural and healthy life which is beneficial in the long run. Professionally too, they do well, especially, in business. They have cheerful and energetic temperaments which make them quite popular.

42
(SINCERE)

This number is a number of charisma, power and destiny. The natives have a strong belief in fate and appeal to the opposite sex. Moneywise, investments yield good returns. The natives also have interest in art, music and drama. They should work on not being overly benevolent but should aim at being more realistic.

51
(MATERIALISTIC)

The influence of the Sun and the planet Mercury bestows the natives with a sharp and keen intellect. Alert and motivated, natives are able to cope with challenges and overcome enmity and rivalry. Professional undertakings are successful and there will not be an extreme shortage of money. The natives must guard against threat to life from mishaps.

60
(HEALER)

The presence of Venus in number 60 endows the natives with growth, rewards and recognition in their professions. From a financial standpoint as well, the natives are quite fortunate and do well in fields of medicine, law and politics. Friends bring happiness, and children bring contentment.

69
(HARMONY)

Number 69 is especially fortunate for men and enables them to reach high positions. Natives are blessed with wisdom and discretion and can use both to achieve personal and professional dreams and goals. The influence of Venus allows the natives to take calculated risks and being a balanced number, creates harmony in their lives as well. Friends and family both love and admire the natives.

78
(UNORGANISED)

This particular number is well suited for those planning to start a family. Natives are emotional and sentimental, which if not balanced with practicality, affect their health and well-being. This also signifies that money is spent in large amounts.

However, there will not be a shortage and natives will lead a comfortable life. When aspected negatively, natives have to overcome obstacles in love and marriage.

87
(Strength)

Number 87 natives need to put in their best efforts in order to achieve their goals and lead a life of comfort and security. There may be ups and downs in their lives but the positive influence of Saturn would bring more optimism into dull days. They are inclined towards religion which gives them a lot of strength. They are also brave and good leaders.

96
(Go-getting)

Creative as well as courageous, number 96 natives have the influence of Mars due to which they are able to realise their ambitions and exploit their talents. They are emotional and hence, the relationships they have play an important role in their personal and professional lives.

105
(Sensuous)

This number is a sign that the natives wish to lead a life of comfort and luxury. Everything that is pleasurable and pleasing to the eye appeal to them, and they are dignified and poised. Being gentle and generous would win the natives friends and popularity in professional and personal circles.

Octave of Number 7

7
(INTUITIVE)

It has the tendency to bestow individuals with certain unique traits. It makes the natives sentimental and their minds are nervous and anxious. Wealth, money, legacies are linked with the presence of Neptune. It can result in arguments and conflicts in a marriage. General weakness and lymphatic disorders are ruled by Neptune.

16
(PEACEMAKER)

Natives of number 16 are peace-loving individuals, who will often mediate and try and bring about order. They are also quite perceptive and are loving people who have lofty goals and aspirations. The position of the Sun in its fall with Venus is quite influential as far as business and professional aspirations are concerned. Natives must also guard against mishaps, rivalries and secret adversaries. Relatives and family members bring them happiness and give them strength to meet hardships and overcome obstacles. They will work well in religious organisations due to their inherent temperaments.

25
(Look-see work)

This particular number is influenced by the Moon and Mercury and the natives are imaginative, mysterious and dreamy. They are interested in spiritualism, religion and occult practices. Initially, they may face difficulties in love and romance, however, they will find loving partners. They believe in helping others and are career-oriented, yet selfless.

34
(Punctilious)

This particular number endows the natives with compassion and kindness and gives them friends who are helpful. This number is also quite lucky for love, romance and marriage and further endows the natives with a sense of spiritualism and religion. They are willing in to put in a lot of hard work and effort in order to achieve goals and fulfil ambitions.

43
(Upheavals)

This number is related to the influence of nature and the combination of Uranus and Jupiter. It brings good fortune to the native and enables them to build a secure future. The natives benefit from buying property situated close to a water body. Negatively aspected, this number can bring many about ups and downs in their lives.

52
(FAITHFUL)

The Moon and Mercury come together in number 52 and give the natives idealistic temperaments and an affinity with nature. They are fond of travelling and are not comfortable with monotony. Change is a key feature of their lives and they are also inclined towards spiritualism. If aspected negatively, there is a threat from water bodies and mishaps.

61
(BENEVOLENT)

The combination of Venus and the Sun in number 61 bestows the natives with sophistication, sentiments and a generous temperament. They will succeed in life, at professional and personal levels. They are also inclined towards travelling and exploring, as well as building a secure future. A word of advice is that they should take utmost advantage of all the opportunities that come their way.

70
(TRAVELLING)

Natives of number 70 are inclined towards the spiritual and philosophical aspects of life. Idealistic and intuitive, they are able to pick up vibrations from others and respond accordingly. Professionally, this is a fortunate number and allows the natives to pursue their goals. Moreover, this also indicates a fair amount of travel and at times, natives may even settle in foreign lands.

79
(CREATIVE)

Number 79 natives are happy, friendly and loving individuals who want newness and adventure in their lives at all times. They also have a sharp business acumen and creative flair and this enables them to profit from a financial standpoint. Independent and freedom loving, they do not like to walk on the beaten track, and would rather make their own path to progress.

88
(POWER AND PEACE)

The influence of double Saturn gives the natives a pious bent of the mind and also ensures that they rise high and make a lot of money. Reticent, wise and hard-working, they also have a generous and kind heart which will win them many friends and well-wishers. Charismatic and convincing, the natives do well in most professions and businesses.

97
(PERSISTENT)

The combination of Mars and Neptune endows the natives with compassion and a humane temperament. Moreover, they have a way with words and are able to express themselves clearly and succinctly. Even though the natives may not have an excellent start in life, they are able to work up the ladder without much effort.

106
(Patience)

Natives of number 106 are restless and want things to happen with speed. Waiting and paying attention to the small things are not their strong points and hence, things may go wrong at times. They must be especially careful in matters of the heart and not get swayed easily. They should also guard against falling prey to flattery and hearsay.

Octave of Number 8

8
(Spiritualism)

This planet is called the 'great misfortune'. If it is badly situated in a horoscope, its adverse effects on the Houses or other planets can be quite fatal. Landed wealth and assets are influenced by Saturn. Natives are gifted with long lives, but have to endure many continual illnesses and ailments.

When the cards are laid out, it symbolises, conceit, capable advice, longevity and endurance.

17
(Thinker)

Number 17 natives are influenced by the Sun and Neptune combination and are intense, passionate and quite philosophical in their outlook. However, at the same time, they are realistic and give importance to the material pleasures of life. Diligence and determination are their key traits, and these lead them to success and good fortune. Most of them tend to be very careful with money and are also wary of new relations. They work well in the fields of medicine, science and minerals. They should guard against court cases and crafty individuals who try to harm them.

26
(SELF CONFIDENCE)

Natives of number 26 are influenced by the Moon and Venus and are intelligent, energetic and successful in most endeavours. They are also gifted with keen perception and make successful astrologers, healers, scientists, doctors and lawyers. Whether aspected positively or negatively, this number brings prosperity, success and growth to the natives. However, they should guard against confusion, misunderstanding and conflict, especially on the domestic front.

35
(CURIOSITY)

Number 35 is a number which endows the natives with intense and profound temperaments. As a result of which, they want to spend time on their own and introspect and reflect on the mysteries of life. They are also academically inclined and hence rise high in society and in their professions. The natives also enjoy travelling and are fortunate in most aspects.

44
(CAUTION)

The combination of double Uranus makes the natives devoted and sincere friends and relatives. They may be inclined towards religion, mysticism and a deeper meaning of life. The desire to achieve a lot would enable them to work hard and rise as high as their hearts aspire to. The natives should exercise caution while dealing with money.

53
(Sympathetic)

If the number 53 is in 10 of Sagittarius, the natives have to work doubly hard to progress and succeed in life. They are able to grow mostly with the aid of influential friends and relatives. However, an inherent strength of mind and body enables them to work hard, thereby clearing the path towards progress.

62
(Tenacious)

Sociable, intelligent and gifted, number 62 natives are influenced by the Moon and Venus. They therefore, make proficient professionals in fields of medicine, law and politics. They are inclined towards literature and the arts and experience glory only after overcoming challenges and putting in hard work. They should guard against investing in speculative ventures.

71
(Suspicious)

Influenced by the vibrations of the Sun and Neptune, number 71 natives are strong-willed and persist in following their goals and dreams to the last point. They may also be affected by the laid-back aspect of Saturn in some cases, and therefore, may not take many risks. Wary and careful, they do not place their trust in people quickly and easily.

80
(LAW BREAKER)

Influenced by the vibrations of Saturn and Pluto, number 80 natives enjoy the company of people. However, they should not indulge in rumour-mongering and gossiping. A philosophical outlook enables them to overcome hardships and learn from them, while their own hard work leads to success and prosperity. They have their own unique outlook on life and do not conform blindly to tradition. They should refrain from indulging in corrupt practices.

89
(ARROGANT)

Number 89 natives need to work on being more strong-willed and active, so as to prevent enemies from overpowering them. They are also somewhat laidback and fatalistic in their attitude. If they learn to face challenges and overcome them, they will progress very smoothly and there will be plenty of success and prosperity in everything that they undertake.

98
(SELF-CENTERED)

Mars and Saturn come together in number 98, enabling the natives to achieve lofty positions in society dependent upon their hard work and intellect. Tender and benevolent, the natives are able to prosper in business as well as professional ventures. Even in their personal lives, relationships are fulfilling. They should pay special attention to health.

107
(PESSIMISM)

This number endows natives with endurance, stamina and mental acumen, because of which they do well as leaders and administrators. However, they should guard against becoming controlling. Being more gentle and considerate will surely help the natives achieve much more in life.

Octave of Number 9

9
(MAGNETIC)

The planet represents a man who attracts women on the basis of his physical strength and ability. Number 9 natives are gifted with gracious and superior characters. They do not hesitate to stand up for those who are weaker than them and will shield them bravely. The natives also do well in other fields, since they have a dependable and solid attitude to life.

18
(DYNAMIC)

These individuals are under the influence of two strong planets, the Sun and Saturn. As a result, their personalities are also strong, self-reliant, and courageous in all aspects. They believe in themselves and are ready to take a stand when needed. They are also attracted towards the opposite sex and also enjoy marital bliss and harmony. Mishaps, injuries and surgeries are risky. This is a number associated with curative powers and bringing about justice. Therefore natives do well in the fields of medicine, law and even religion.

27
(TRAIL BLAZER)

Number 27 natives are influenced by the Moon and Neptune and hence, have a strong sense of fairness and are honest and straightforward in everything they do. They do well in fields of administration, government offices and politics. Benevolent and compassionate, they share their time and money willingly. They are also determined and dynamic, and experience great fortune in their latter years.

36
(DILIGENT)

This number is fortunate for the individual in more ways than one, and though the natives have to put in a lot of hard work, the rewards are assured. Because of their temperament, the natives make good administrators or senior executives and are also able to lead a life of comfort and contentment at home.

45
(ACTIVITY)

This number endows the natives with a happy-go-lucky attitude and a sociable outlook. Therefore, they have many friends who are supportive and encouraging. In matters of marriage, the natives may benefit from a financial standpoint. Brimming with vitality and confidence enables them to deal with any challenge whatsoever.

54
(Name and Fame)

In number 54, the influence of Mercury is ten times greater than that of Uranus. As a result, the natives have discretion and sharp minds which enable them to aim for lofty ambitions and also realise them. They however, need to focus on organisational skills and not get disappointed if success, fame and fortune do not come easily.

63
(Noble)

Natives of this number are helped by friends and relatives in the journey to success. The influence of Venus ensures a smooth love life and the happiness of children as well as a sparkling social life. If the native is a man, he will be attractive for women who will help him emotionally and financially. Faithfulness and determination bring benefits in the long run.

72
(High position)

For number 72 natives, being influenced by the vibrations of Neptune and the Moon, financial matters are affected and the individual's diligence determine his prosperity. Natives enjoy travelling on water and also shine in social circles. Marriage is a little late on the cards; however, will be a happy union. Benevolent and helpful, natives are also helped by associates and friends.

81
(ENERGETIC)

The combination of Saturn and Sun is a powerful one and therefore, the natives are influential and intelligent. They are charitable and sociable and have an interest in the mystic and mysterious. Money increases after the age of thirty-six. Natives should guard against losing their tempers quickly.

90
(STRONG WILLED)

The influence of the planet Mars in mid-heaven is strong and this ensures that the natives can carry out the riskiest of ventures with ease and efficiency. Politics, law and business suit them and they are able to efficiently deal with challenges. Authority suits the natives, and in matters of love and romance, they are passionate and intense.

99
(PRUDENT)

The presence of Jupiter in number 99 endows natives with a positive frame of mind and they are able to deal with life with wisdom, emotion and diligence. Their ambitions and desires do not go against their moral fabric and hence, are possible and realistic. This number is also inclined towards travelling, especially, on the professional front. Religion too, is an important part of their lives.

108
(A SUPREME POWER)

This particular number is quite favourable provided the Sun is placed well in the House; in which case, the natives are gifted mentally and are perceptive, intuitive and intelligent. Coping with life on a day to day basis is easy and so is planning for the future. This number also endows the natives with the ability to take on responsibility professionallies and succeed at all levels. This number, indeed, is a number of strength and influence.

Monthly Forecasts

In this system one has to consider the date, the month and the year in one's birth date. In this, one has to add the number of the current month and the number of months after one's last birth date. For example if one's date of birth is 18-05-1952 and the current month is July 2007.

Calculation Method

1.	Your date of birth	18
2.	Your month of birth	5
3.	Year of your birth	1952
4.	No of current month	7
5.	No of months from your last birthday	2
	Total	1984

Reduce this total to a single digit which is 4. Thus, the month July 2007 would be a 4 individual month circle. Please read the explanation given for number 4.

NUMBER 1

It's a month of ups and downs, and depending the way they respond to new erotica, their emotional graph will be a see-saw. They should avoid spending on other people more lavishly than they deserve and should not deny themselves stuff either. They should be dependable without having to suffer or bend backwards in the process. Their hearts will be full of joy and contentment, thanks to a person in their immediate surroundings. Alternatively, their current state of bliss could even come from being single! They'll have to go easy on the excitement as their heart and imagination may actually be doing more for them than the people themselves. If they are learning their life lessons well, they will get rewarded handsomely. Speculative trading should be avoided. They should meet as many new people as possible. They should put off particularly taxing work in the last quarter.

LUCKY DATES	:	4, 13, 22, 31
LUCKY DAYS	:	Mondays and Fridays
ARTICLES FOR DONATION	:	Gur, channa dal

NUMBER 2

The area of their personal income and values is on the agenda for them this month. There is a momentum towards their future success as a lot of energy is being applied toward this. They will be mentally recapping whatever they have learned, that could help them conserve and increase their personal resources. Their emotions could get in the way and cover the reality of things. A friend or acquaintance could be involved in all this and they may also bring some constructive and innovative ideas that they could use in the future. They develop more maturity in the way they communicate, and their talent and charm could come to the forefront this month, in any interchange, especially at the home base. Changes and promotion are on the cards.

LUCKY DATES   : 5, 14, 23
LUCKY DAYS   : Tuesday
ARTICLES FOR DONATION : Red cloth

NUMBER 3

This will be an intense month with emotions running high. It's up to them to keep calm and resolve conflicts. Chartered accountants and financial advisors have to be extremely careful. New work proposals are worth considering. They will gain vigour and vitality. They should not invest in fresh ventures. Students will emerge successful in their tests/interviews. Their input will be appreciated by loved ones who have made mistakes. Later in the month, an urge may compel them to experience deeper personal interactions within relationships, either existing ones or new ones. This could seem to be a fleeting feeling or a part of their ongoing search for meaning. Family life tends to suffer due to their unreasonable and fiery temper. Caution is advised while dealing with new clients.

LUCKY DATES   : 1, 10, 19, 28
LUCKY DAYS   : Wednesday and Friday
ARTICLES FOR DONATION : Mah saboot, mustard oil

NUMBER 4

This month, they will appreciate the intellectually stimulating atmosphere that will prevail at work. They need to be careful as they are accident-prone. Politicians are likely to come under public gaze. They should plan out their budget and it would be wise to stick to it. Their partners will be emotionally and financially supportive. Everyone they meet will teach them something new and interesting and they will try to bring this knowledge to more productive use. They will earn good money at work, but will have difficulty in collecting their earnings. For some, a change of residence, purchase of a car or an overseas journey will be high on the cards. Elders and children in the family will demand more attention. In the end of the month, travelling for business will not only bring them valuable information, but monetary benefits as well.

LUCKY DATES   : 9, 18, 27
LUCKY DAYS   : Sunday and Tuesday
ARTICLES FOR DONATION : Rice, sugar

NUMBER 5

Life is a big party this month. They'll have energy for everything except constructive work and this can cause stress in the family. They should try to get a head start in their career. Law and management students will have a tough time as they take longer to grasp things. Friends will admire their scholastic abilities, but secretly hope that they amount to nothing. They will imagine they are in love at least half a dozen times this month. They should hold on to all that they have. A Leo friend could cause a rift between them and their loved ones. Delightful times lie ahead with picnics and lots of opportunities for relaxation. They will make rapid strides in the social scene and become a rage more popular than boy bands and girl bands.

LUCKY DATES   : 6, 12, 15, 30
LUCKY DAYS   : Monday and Friday
ARTICLES FOR DONATION : Donate green cloth to a poor woman.

NUMBER 6

The prevailing tone of this month is a mix of conflicting energies that might put a bit of stress on them, but it is nothing they can't handle. In fact, if anyone is going to make the most out of the month, it will be them. They should tap into their aggressive nature and act boldly towards the object of their desire. At the same time, they should make sure that there is harmony amongst those around them and make sure everyone's needs are taken care of so that peace may exist among all. They're popular and make new contacts easily. The future seems bright when they have something to look forward to. They are happier working at their own pace, without too much supervision. They should avoid group pressures for the time being, and join them again later in the month.

LUCKY DATES   : 9, 18, 27
LUCKY DAYS   : Tuesday and Thursday
ARTICLES FOR DONATION : Donate 1 ¼ kgs of wheat on Tuesday

NUMBER 7

A confrontation should be avoided this month. Loans, ceremonies, marriages and the birth of a child will be the highlights of this month. For working girls, transfer is indicated to a place of their choice. Monetary problems will be nagging them. Eventually, it will be a satisfying period where support from people around them would give them strength to complete their plans. Their talents would surface at social gatherings. Those in real estate or land development will fine tune an idea and earn money and goodwill. Some of them have been toying with the idea of building a home for destitutes, and the time is just right to put this plan into action. Poets, cine artists and film producers will have excellent opportunities to sign new contracts.

LUCKY DATES : 1, 10, 20
LUCKY DAYS : Wednesday and Friday
ARTICLES FOR DONATION : Donate 1¼ kgs of moong saboot at place of worship.

NUMBER 8

They have a lot of pleasant surprises coming their way, that have nothing to do with what they deserve. They will be delighted and, after a point, be surprised at the way things are turning out right. People close to their hearts will be patient, loving and sweet. Parents may disapprove of wild parties or bad company. Love can take a few knocks due to misunderstandings. A Leo or Piscean friend blows hot and cold, but eventually turns out to be lukewarm. There's no knowing how much of what they say will be registered by those who claim to love them, so they should keep things light instead of getting too intense and involved. Friends should not be told any secrets. Journalists, publishers, writers and those dealing with iron, leather and steel will have many opportunities for expansion in business.

LUCKY DATES : 6, 15, 24
LUCKY DAYS : Wednesday and Sunday
ARTICLES FOR DONATION : Donate sugar and rice (1 ¼ kgs each) at place of worship.

NUMBER 9

This month, most of their time will be consumed at the professional front, and they will be engaged in solving a tricky problem. There are indications that they are likely to be entrusted with the responsibility of solving a complaint. It would be in their interest to take appropriate action against subordinates if an inquiry finds them guilty. However, the aim should also be to try to build a better organisational culture in their department. A suitable matrimonial proposal for their eligible son/daughter is also foreseen. Models and cine artists are in the limelight. For private employees, their silence will prove more harmful. They should take care while driving, especially on Tuesdays and Saturdays. Military personnel and police officers whose professions have a particular attire will have an excellent month. Airhostesses, airlines staff and restaurant owners will have a good time.

LUCKY DATES : 3, 12, 21, 30
LUCKY DAYS : Wednesday and Saturday
ARTICLES FOR DONATION : Channa dal and turmeric

Yearly Forecasts

In this system, we have to consider the date and the month of the birthdate. One has to add the number of the current year. Fox example if the date of birth is 18-05 and the current year 2007:

Date of birth	18
Month of birth	5
Current year	2007
Total	2030

Reduce this total to a single digit which is 5. Thus, the year 2007 would be a 5 individual year circle. Please read the explanation given in number 5.

NUMBER 1

An amazing placement of the Sun promises that the coming year will be a landmark year in their lives. This year, they will get fame and authority. They will scale greater heights in their careers and achieve financial affluence hitherto only dreamt of. They will be confident of everything they do. They will be assertive and communicative. Behind the scene activities and matters related to siblings will also come to the forefront. They will see life differently and make plans for the future. Expenses are, like the previous year, still more than the comfort level. Healthwise, they need to take care in the months of May-June.

Overall, it is advisable that new investments/projects are not undertaken and old projects are given full attention. It is most important to exercise utmost caution in money matters and keep relations with relatives balanced. Major changes around the month of October will make life even more comfortable. Those married will share good understanding and rapport with their mates.

LUCKY DATES	: 4, 13, 22
LUCKY DAYS	: Friday and Saturday
ARTICLES FOR DONATION	: Black cloth, mah saboot

NUMBER 2

The year shows hard work but at the same time, certain progress in their careers and business. They will have to be constantly alert for any opportunity that comes along. It is an auspicious year for renovation and foreign travel. There will not be any sudden gains and they will have to remain content with the slow rate of growth. They should not get lured by quick profit schemes, for these will result in a financial setback. The months they need to watch out are May-June and October. They should try to work independently, even though progress appears slow. The employed will benefit by sticking to their current jobs and not seeking a change. The married and also lovers will face occasional fights and emotional setbacks which will slowly make them drift apart. Most of them may have the tendency to put on weight, and it seems they will certainly add a couple of extra kilos. They need to take care of their health especially during the months of July, September and December. There is no major problem, but there is no harm in being extra careful during these months. Overall, the coming year is one of struggle, but one which will take them much closer to their goals.

LUCKY DATES   : 5, 14, 23
LUCKY DAYS   : Wednesday, Friday and Sunday
ARTICLES FOR DONATION : Oil, coal

NUMBER 3

They can look forward to a year of progress and prosperity. The more ambitious they are, the more success and glory comes their way. They are, by nature, cautious and practical and even in their wildest dreams, they do not lose their practical approach to life. This characteristic in their nature will assure them safe passage through an occasional rough patch that they may encounter in their business and careers. The months, May/June/September/October will test their ingenuity, when they are confronted with tricky situations in their work. They will certainly come out of the difficult patch, but after suffering a minor, but bearable loss. The employed will make rapid progress in their careers with their work. Sincere appreciation from their seniors and employers is to be expected. It is quite understandable that the accolades they receive will raise their expectations for a major promotion.

LUCKY DATES   : 1, 10, 19, 21
LUCKY DAYS   : Thursday and Friday
ARTICLES FOR DONATION : Sugar, ghee, white cloth

NUMBER 4

They will start the year mixing business with pleasure and despite important developments on the relationship front, they really can't take away their attention from their careers. Fortunate Jupiter is in their zone of their relationships, it is difficult to avoid the conclusion that it is now or never for at least one important personal or commercial relationship. Their domestic situation or financial pressures may influence the desire to know where they stand. Some of them will find the demands of children difficult at times, especially with so much good opportunities appearing to pass them by. For others, people they meet socially may be keen to get intimate with them while hoping not to make commitments or promises themselves. This could come to a head in autumn if they've been giving themselves away too easily or too eagerly. They'll have to redress the balance if they're ignoring their own needs and possibly those of their family.

LUCKY DATES   : 2, 22, 30
LUCKY DAYS   : Sunday, Monday and Wednesday
ARTICLES FOR DONATION : Masoor dal, sugar

NUMBER 5

Stars are extra helpful, and all being well, the year promises to be excellent for financial gains and career growth. Few new opportunities will invoke new confidence and enthusiasm in them. They should not be highly outspoken and reveal their future plans to others. Unexpected gains could be through speculation, and will put them in a very comfortable position. They will spend lavishly, not only on themselves, but also on their family members and friends. Youngsters will get to know someone very interesting and an exciting romance especially in the months of May, June, September and October is expected. Students are assured smooth sailing, and with a little bit of effort, they will achieve wonderful results in exams and sports. Their health will be good and they will be full of vitality throughout this year.

LUCKY DATES : 4, 13, 22
LUCKY DAYS : Tuesday and Saturday
ARTICLES FOR DONATION : Moong saboot, green cloth

NUMBER 6

The next twelve months will see them rather busy and they will be running around to keep abreast with competition in their business and careers. However, it will be a successful year, but only after they put in a lot of hard work and struggle. They may have had it easy so far, but not any longer. Their work will require full time attention and any neglect or slip up could set them back several months, if not years. They cannot afford to take it easy nor can they take risk it in ventures about which they may have little or no knowledge at all. Business people will concentrate all their energies in achieving a breakthrough in the international arena, and may even succeed in getting a foothold in the overseas market. Their efforts will certainly bear fruits around the months of March/ July/August and October. There will be frequent travels abroad for business or work that may even lead them to consider setting up an office or base in a foreign country.

LUCKY DATES   : 6, 15, 24
LUCKY DAYS   : Friday and Saturday
ARTICLES FOR DONATION : Ghee, gur, camphor

NUMBER 7

This year, they can turn almost any situation to their best advantage. Good health and a happy family life is assured in the first half. Fresh projects started before 15 April do not yield much returns. The family front seems good and they can expect full cooperation from their brothers, sisters and spouses. In spite of a hectic and regular travel schedule that they might follow this year, they will enjoy visiting new places and meeting new people. People of marriageable age get married in the second quarter. Some misunderstanding can arise between couples in June-July, so adequate care should be taken in such matters during this period. Windfall gains may be expected in April, May and September for poets, journalists and media persons. An increase in work related hurdles might be experienced in November and December.

LUCKY DATES   : 3, 20, 30
LUCKY DAYS   : Wednesday and Sunday
ARTICLES FOR DONATION : Rice, oil and black cloth

NUMBER 8

The year seems to be highly significant for those in the field of education, sports, computers and medicine. A career change is in the offing for most of them. Social engagements will keep them busy. Their faith in the future, quest for knowledge and belief in themselves will pay big dividends and enable them to face the coming year with conviction. A property transaction or acquiring a new vehicle seems very likely around September. The months of February, May and October will be highly significant. This year is fantastic for career growth, so they should not miss any opportunity to show their talents and to shine brightly in the eyes of their seniors. For those in business, this period does not ensure rewards immediately, but eventually gains will be much beyond their expectations. New assignments and contracts will be signed which will prove beneficial in the long run. Support from their co-workers and partners will help in achieving goals. They should avoid investment until they have consulted experts.

LUCKY DATES   : 5, 14, 23
LUCKY DAYS   : Thursday
ARTICLES FOR DONATION : Milk, sugar

NUMBER 9

Their home and family life seem rather comfortable throughout the year. The married will travel frequently in the company of their spouses and beloved to their favourite holiday resort. They can look forward to romantic togetherness during the summer and winter vacations. The months of July and August sees a slight health problem for their partners and this could cause lot of anxiety. Students come under very favourable planetary influence this year for their education and sports activities. They can set their target high, both in studies as well as in their careers, for they are certain to achieve their goals this year. Those who are keen on losing weight will achieve remarkable results by following a regime of light physical exercise and dietary control. In fact, some of them could be affected by illnesses causing alarm in the family. They are advised not to overdo weight reduction, for they could end up having more health problems. Overall, they can look forward to another year of positive results.

LUCKY DATES	: 7, 16, 25
LUCKY DAYS	: Sunday and Tuesday
ARTICLES FOR DONATION	: Green cloth, moong dal and green vegetables